Gerald Thorne

Heaven on Earth

A realistic tale

Gerald Thorne

Heaven on Earth
A realistic tale

ISBN/EAN: 9783337089085

Printed in Europe, USA, Canada, Australia, Japan

Cover: Foto ©Andreas Hilbeck / pixelio.de

More available books at **www.hansebooks.com**

HEAVEN ON EARTH.

A

REALISTIC TALE.

BY

GERALD THORNE.

~~~~~~

NEW YORK:

LOVELL BROTHERS & COMPANY,

141-155 EAST 25TH STREET.

CONTENTS.

CHAPTER.   PAGE.

PREFACE.   5

I. INTRODUCING MR. SCOTT, - - - - - -   9

II. A BIT OF HISTORY, - - - - - - -   31

III. THE SPIRITUAL SCHOOL, - - - - - -   41

IV. THE NEW HOME, - - - - - - - -   48

V. OUT OF THE WORLD, - - - - - - -   55

VI. THE EVENING MEETING, - - - - -   66

VII. MR. SCOTT FINDS EMPLOYMENT, - - -   78

VIII. SOCIAL FORCES, - - - - - - - -   94

IX. A MODEL EXCURSION, - - - - - - - 105

X. THE TOBACCO PRINCIPALITY, - - - - 118

XI. COMPLEX LOVE, - - - - - -   - - 125

XII. AN ACCIDENT, - - - - - - - - 144

XIII. A FALSE INSPIRATION, - - - - - - 158

XIV. THE LAST ENEMY, - - - - - - - 175

XV. THE CHILDREN, - - - - - - - - 186

XVI. A NOTABLE LECTURE, - - - - - - 195

XVII. MODERN NICODEMUSES, - - - - - - 208

XVIII. MR. SCOTT'S DECISION, - - - - - - 223

PREFACE.

The veriest tyro in social science may see, in the agitations and upheavals which constantly convulse society, evidences that the world is outgrowing its old forms and customs, which no longer meet its requirements, and that the forces of progress, which have been so long held back, are ready to burst forth and create for themselves a new social system.

WHAT SHALL THAT SYSTEM BE?

Shall the coming social revolution be a peaceful and noble one, guided by an enlightened scientific opinion, and leading up to an enormous increase of human happiness, or shall we, by attempting to still longer enslave mankind under the selfish system which has produced such deep misery among the masses, and which is dominated, not by science, but by hoary traditions; shall we, I ask, so dam up these grow-

ing forces that when they do break
loose it will be to the destruction of
much that is good?

In the following chapters the author
has ventured to suggest what might
prove to be a better way of life. He
realizes that to have done this without
much regard to present public opinion
is a very bold thing. But with an
earnest purpose to give expression to
those principles which he believes are
destined ultimately to triumph in this
world, nay, which *must* triumph before
we can cease to be hypocrites and live
according to our prayers and professions, bold things become justifiable.

The experiences here related may be
taken as a suggestion of what can certainly be done, at any time, by any
number, and in any land, *provided selfishness can be subdued*, and a spirit of
unity and love be accepted as the true
basis of all good social organization.

The author would feel a peculiar
gratification if those who thoughtfully
read this little book will in some way
record their verdict as to the desirable-

ness of studying out a new and more
scientific order of society, with some
brief expression of their views as to
what the new life should be. He cordially invites criticism of his own ideas.
Would you not prefer such a social
system as is here outlined to the present one?

GERALD THORNE.

NEW YORK, April 15th, 1896.

CHAPTER I.

IT was near the close of a mild day in the latter part of May, 18—, that the steamship *Majestic* sailed up the splendid harbor of New York and was slowly and carefully warped into her berth. Her promenade deck was occupied by a crowd of the cabin passengers, each anxious to catch a first view of friends awaiting them on shore. Many were the signals, as one after another was recognized. Handkerchiefs waved, and kisses were thrown back and forth, from ship to pier and from pier to ship. A young wife actually fainted from the strain of suspense, before her husband was able to land and clasp her to his breast.

Among the passengers was one who had remained calm and seemingly unmoved. He was a pleasant-looking man, apparently about thirty-five years of age, rather above the middle height,

erect, spare in flesh, with almost a mili-
tary bearing. This was Mr. George
Alexander Scott, a native of New York,
who had been spending some years in
Europe. Mr. Scott was a bachelor, and
having neither wife nor children to
greet him on his return to his native
land, he was spared the intense emotions
of his fellow-passengers, while realising
that milder feeling of pleasure which
every one experiences on returning
home. Expecting no one to welcome
him, great was his surprise and joy
when, on marching down the gang-
plank, the first person he met was his
cousin Louise, now Mrs. Reginald Vincent, of whom he had always been very
fond. They had been much together
in childhood, but he had not seen her
for several years, and meantime she had
married. Learning that he had sailed
on the *Majestic*, she had driven down
to meet him.

He grasped her hand and kissed her
affectionately.

"Come," she said, "you are going
right home with me. I have come

down on purpose to get you. How well you are looking, George! You haven't grown old a bit."

" I was just thinking the same thing of you," he said; "you always were a comely maid, but now that you have bloomed out into wifehood you are sweeter than ever."

Mrs. Vincent blushed a little at this hearty compliment, and bade him make haste to get his luggage past the customs officers. This occupied but a few minutes, when they immediately entered the carriage and were driven rapidly up-town to her handsome residence on Madison Avenue. Here Mr. Scott took up his domicile for a time, enjoying the hospitality of his cousin and her husband, who, by the way, was a rising young lawyer.

A few days later Mrs. Vincent invited the Rev. Mr. Langford and his wife to dine with her. Mr. Langford was a distant relative, who would, she thought, be pleased to meet their guest. At this dinner, after Mr. Scott had given them a brief account of his travels abroad, he was moved to make some rather warm expressions of satisfaction at once more being with friends in his native city. This seemed to strike a responsive chord in Mrs. Vincent's heart, for she exclaimed:

"I am very glad to hear you speak thus, George; I should think you would be tired of roaming about the world as you have been doing. You ought to marry and settle down where we can see more of you. Just reflect that you are becoming almost a stranger to those of your own flesh and blood."

"I should have tired of the roaming long ago," he replied, "if I had not had a purpose other than pleasure-seeking. I have been making rather a serious study of the different peoples I have been amongst, so the time has not seemed long."

"Pray tell us what phases of life you were particularly interested in studying," said Mr. Vincent. "Your observations ought to be valuable."

"The laws and customs of different nations vary greatly," replied Mr. Scott, "yet each seems to consider its own ways the best—at least, for its own people. I wanted to observe them all and see which I thought was best."

"Well, I suppose you reached some satisfactory conclusions, did you not?"

"Yes. In material progress and inventions our own favored nation leads the world. In some other respects we are too complacent; we might learn much of the older nations. But, looking at the condition of the people, there are many things in every form of society I have seen which are so faulty and productive of evil that I am inclined to think a more scientific system than any of the old ones may yet be devised."

"What faults have you discovered in the better classes of English society and in our own people?" asked the Rev. Mr. Langford.

"In studying social science we must take into consideration the state of a whole nation and not select the favored classes," answered Mr. Scott. "Everywhere on the earth we find the rich and the poor; on the one hand, those

who cannot spend their princely incomes, though they indulge in every
known luxury; on the other hand, those
who are unable to procure enough food
to keep themselves and their little ones
from starving. This comes from our
living in a system of competition where
each strives with his fellow for the
possession of wealth. Of course, the
strong and capable overcome the weak
and ignorant. The private or individual ownership of property is at the
bottom of it all."

"But, surely," said Mr. Langford,
"you would not advocate a general
equalising of wealth. That could only
be done by overthrowing our whole
existing system of laws, and exercising
force or compulsion, which would be,
in effect, robbery. That is the doctrine
of the socialists and anarchists, is it
not?"

"Yes," said Mr. Vincent, "that
would land us in a bad state of things.
And even if wealth were to be so
equalised it would not remain equal
a day. Trading would commence, and

some would gain while others lost; so we would, after a time, be back where we are now, with the rich and poor as you have described them."

"I have no thought of advocating any such forcible equalisation of wealth," said Mr. Scott. "You will have to admit, however, will you not, that the present system brings about great suffering and hardship among the masses."

"Yes," said Mr. Langford, "that is undeniable. But no better system has ever been devised, so we have to put up with the evils of the present one."

"Have you ever tried to devise a better system?" asked Mr. Scott.

"No, I confess I have not. It seems to me that if any better social system were possible it would have been discovered long ago."

"I do not see that that follows. It may be that too much has been taken for granted, and that not enough study has been given the matter. Some prophet may yet arise who will point out to us better ways of life. I do not wish to be misunderstood as advocating any of the foolish ideas of the so-called socialists. So long as we have all stood by consenting to the selfish old game of competition, and even taking part in it, we must accept the results without complaining. But we have an unquestionable right to adopt better ways as soon as we discover them. As population steadily increases, competition becomes more severe, and the consequent misery of the less capable increases. There are plenty of signs nowadays that the strain of the game is becoming too great to be borne. The leaning towards governmental control of telegraphs, railroads, etc., merely shows a desire to limit competition and escape from the power of concentrated capital. The jealousy of trusts and monopolies arises from the same feeling."

"It seems to me," said Mr. Vincent, "that the tendency to paternalism in government only works mischief. The freer competition can be left the better for all."

"So it seems to me," said Mr. Langford. "There can be no such thing as establishing an equality of fortune, and it is folly to expect it. We shall always have the poor with us, and they must learn to be reconciled to the circumstances in which Providence has seen fit to place them. Unless they take that attitude anarchy will come in."

"Is there not still another way?" asked Mr. Scott. "Suppose a general change of feeling could be brought about, such that loftier sentiments would take the place of selfish desires of ownership, and would lead the rich to voluntarily share with the poor, not in any pinched or niggardly way, but so as to elevate and refine them, and make them all comfortable and happy. If a new order of society could be devised which would bring about such results, one that both rich and poor would choose to enter without the slightest compulsion, merely because they would be happier in it, it seems to me a new and wonderful step would have been made in the world's progress."

" That is something we are not likely to see in our day," said the Rev. Mr. Langford. " It is altogether visionary and impracticable."

" I am not so sure of that. A new social system may yet be discovered or invented which will have such advantages, and be so attractive, that we shall all make haste to get into it. The desire to acquire greater wealth than one really needs is rather an ignoble one, when you come to seriously weigh it."

" What other radical faults have you found in our present system, besides the inequality of wealth?" asked Mrs. Vincent.

" The institution of marriage seems to carry with it a long train of evils," replied Mr. Scott.

Mr. Langford had given but little attention to social questions, and was like very many others who are apt to think that any deviation from old ways is morally wrong, especially if it concerns the relation of the sexes; so he now spoke up with some severity in his manner.

"What you say suggests strongly that you are in a general quarrel with society. It is all in line with the ideas of foreign agitators, who would, if they could, destroy all law and order. I am surprised that you should say such things. Marriage is a divinely ordained institution, and a great safeguard, whatever may be said against it."

Mrs. Vincent seemed quite worried by the turn the conversation was taking. She had a deep regard for Mr. Scott, and she realised that as he was her guest he was entitled to her protection. So she said:

"I am sure, Mr. Langford, that we shall find cousin George on the right side of these questions when we have heard him through."

"Thank you, cousin," said Mr. Scott, smiling; "Mr. Langford's remarks show the way the average man looks at these matters. It does not follow that one is an enemy of society because he sees the glaring evils of our present system and desires to find some better way."

"That is true," said Mr. Langford, in

a more quiet tone. "The difficulty lies in finding any better way which is really safe and practical. It has never yet been done, and I see nothing to indicate that it is likely to be, however much we may desire it. We shall have to wait for the millennium."

"Until recently I have been forced to take the same hopeless view that you do," said Mr. Scott; "but not very long ago I made a discovery which has interested me greatly. I had not intended to speak of it until I had investigated the matter thoroughly, but our discussion has gone so far that I believe I will tell you about it. Let me say, first, that anyone who studies history, and observes how all laws and customs have been modified by time, will realize that there is no such sacred fixity of institutions as is generally supposed. Everything changes slowly to suit the changing conditions of mankind, and as some nations are more intelligent and progressive than others, the laws and customs of no two are alike.

"To show the changes wrought by

time, take, for example, the statement
that King Solomon had seven hundred
wives, princesses, and three hundred
concubines. There is nothing to show
that either God or man was displeased
with him for this; in fact, it seems to
have been part of the greatness conferred upon him along with his wisdom.
It was only when he went after strange
women, and was influenced by them to
set up strange gods, that he did wrong.
Since then customs and laws have
changed so that in our time, and in our
present system, a man may have only
one wife, be he king or peasant. So
feudalism and slavery have flourished
and afterwards disappeared. In one
country the eldest child now inherits all,
or nearly all, the property of his parents;
in another the youngest takes most; in
still other countries the children inherit
equally. In one country it is almost
impossible to annul a marriage or get a
divorce, while in another a husband
may send his wife back to her parents
whenever he is dissatisfied with her, no
judicial separation being necessary. In

one country, when a man dies, his
widow is, or used to be, burned on the
funeral pyre; while in most other countries she marries another man and is
comforted. These are familiar facts.
I mention them to show that the world
is not chained down to any one form,
but is constantly changing and progressing. Observing this, I asked myself
some time ago: 'What would be an
ideal form of society?' Did you ever
stop to ask yourself that question?"

"I have not opened my mind to any
such speculations, there being no possible profit in it," said Mr. Langford.

"The thought never even occurred
to me," remarked Mr. Vincent.

"I have not asked myself such a
question, that is certain," said Mrs.
Vincent. "We ladies have enough to
occupy our time without taking up
matters that only philosophers and lawyers could settle."

"That is true enough," chimed in
Mrs. Langford. "Besides, until the
men will yield us the right to vote, they
deserve to be oppressed by old customs.

I hope I may live to see woman take her proper place as the equal of man."

"Hurrah!" exclaimed Mr. Scott. "I am glad to find one of you who is not wholly satisfied with the present system. It encourages me to tell you the interesting discovery I referred to just now. While I was studying these subjects, and wondering if I could do anything to help bring about necessary changes, such as would do away with our present evils, I chanced to learn that others, more advanced than I, had already undertaken an experiment with a view to establishing a perfect social system. This has now been in progress for years and is very successful thus far. Would you like me to tell you about it?"

"I daresay I have heard of it," said Mr. Langford. "Still, I should be glad to hear your account."

"I will tell you the facts as I have learned them," said Mr. Scott, "and you can each form your own opinion as I have formed mine.

"It is now many years since Mr.

Robert Temple, or 'Father Temple,' as his followers choose to call him, undertook to establish a model society, fashioned on what he conceived to be the heavenly order.   In regard to property he took for his standard the example of the primitive church, as described in the Acts, where it says: 'And all that believed were together and had all things common; and sold their possessions and goods, and parted them to all men, as every man had need.   And the multitude of them that believed were of one heart and one soul: neither said any of them that aught of the things he possessed was his own, but they had all things common.'

" Reasoning on this wonderful record, Father Temple taught that the influence of the Holy Spirit everywhere is to destroy *selfishness*, and that when God's will shall be done on earth as it is in heaven there will be no selfish ownerships, but mankind will become like the believers on the day of Pentecost; that there will then be neither rich nor poor, but all will be supplied according to their needs."

"Did he get any really worthy, respectable people to join in such a movement and put in all their property?" asked Mrs. Vincent.

"I believe some of his people were professional, others were of the middle-class, well-to-do farmers, carpenters, blacksmiths, printers, etc.; nearly all of the trades being represented," replied Mr. Scott.

"Were these people church members before they were converted to the ideas of this man Temple?" asked Mr. Langford.

"Yes, most of them were. Some were Presbyterians, others Congregationalists, Methodists, Episcopalians, etc. They seem to have been a very good sort of people, for they all joined hands in the most fraternal way when they entered the new church, and they claim that their old differences of creeds and ordinances have not troubled one of them since."

"Do they believe in marriage?" inquired Mr. Langford.

"They do not," replied Mr. Scott. "Remember that they have built up their society with the idea of allowing selfishness no place in it. They began by having a common faith, then advanced by putting all their property into a common fund; but it was found that selfishness still lurked in the family relation; so they put away all marriage claims, that no one might say, 'This is *my* wife,' or 'This is *my* husband.'"

On hearing this statement all four of Mr. Scott's listeners began to look very serious. Mr. Langford felt certain of his suspicions confirmed, and decided that it was his duty to open Mr. Scott's eyes to the dangers that lurked in such schemes for social regeneration. Mrs. Vincent judged from the looks of the others that there might be something disagreeable coming, so she hastened to take the helm again.

"Where and when and how did you learn all this, George?" she asked. "You have spent most of your time abroad for some years, yet you tell us news of what has been going on at home."

"I first learned of this society by finding a complete set of their publications in the British Museum. They excited my interest, and I read most of them. The ideas were so in line with my own thoughts that I determined that when I returned to New York, one of the first things I would do would be to visit this society."

"I am astonished that you should meditate such a thing," said the Rev. Mr. Langford in a grave tone of voice, while Mrs. Langford drew her chair a little closer to the side of her husband. "It is all well enough to read about and discuss such matters by way of keeping up with the times, but I consider that it would be going very far to actually visit such a society. It would, in a manner, be recognizing their new system as on a level with ours, and would tend to give them new confidence that their ideas may ultimately be accepted."

"If that is true I certainly will go," said Mr. Scott, dryly. "I have become so interested in the ideas of these

people and their work, that if I find
them to be what I hope and expect, I
may cast my lot with them and join the
society."

At this all his listeners laughed
heartily. It struck them that their
credulity was being imposed upon.
Mr. Scott, however, was evidently
quite serious in what he said. He
begged them to listen to him a little
further, and continued thus:

"It seems to be difficult for you to
conceive of a man in my position taking such a step, but I assure you it is
exactly in line with my deepest con-
victions. I want to do some good in
the world before I die, and I look upon
these people as heroes. They are certainly worthy of respectful study, having
made a more altruistic effort than either
of us has ever made."

"Yes, but, George, think of your large
property! Are you going to risk that
in such a radical experiment?" asked
Mrs. Vincent.

"I shall do nothing rashly. The
visit I propose will do no harm; but if

I find these people to be what I expect,
I shall not hesitate to join them if they
will receive me."

" Let me venture a suggestion," said
..lr. Vincent. " It will be only exercising common prudence for you to try it
a year on probation, before parting with
all your property. I presume they
would take you in that way, and you
would then have ample opportunity to
study the system as you desire, without
taking unnecessary risks."

" That is a good idea," said the Rev.
Mr. Langford. "As a probationary
member Mr. Scott will not share in any
of their possible disasters, while he will
get his eyes open to the fallacies of their
system. These socialistic movements
are all alike, and all are equally certain
to end in failure. By the way, what is
the name of this model society from
which you expect so much?"

" It is called 'The Society of the
Perfect Life.'"

" I have never heard of it," said Mr.
Langford.

" If cousin George is determined to

go and spend a year with these people
on probation," said Mrs. Vincent,
" would it not be a good idea for us all
to meet here again at the expiration of
the time and hear his report. Will you
not be willing, George, to give us the
benefit of your experience so that we
may not have to go through it ourselves ? "

" Most certainly; but it may prove so
attractive that you will wish to go
through it. I will not pledge myself
not to join the society within the year.
My life is more important to me than
to others, and a year is a considerable
part of it; so I shall do what seems
wisest. But I will return at the end of
the year and report to you what I have
found, if my life is spared."

" Very well, then," said Mrs. Vincent;
" you will all dine with me again a year
from now, when I send you notice of
cousin George's return;" and with that
the party broke up.

CHAPTER II.

A BIT OF HISTORY.

Whenever a man does anything out of the ordinary course his motives and purposes are very apt to be misconstrued; so, before we accompany Mr. Scott to the home of the Perfect Life, the reader ought to learn a little more fully how that home came to be established. Where did its founder get his inspiration? Were his motives good or bad? Was his religion genuine, or was his movement only a cleverly devised scheme for selfish ends? These are things we ought to know at the outset, to enable us to form sound opinions as we go along.

Robert Temple was born of a good New England family, and being a bright lad, he was sent to college at an early age, where he graduated with honor. He then chose the legal pro-

fession.   As there were no law schools
in those days, he went through the
prescribed course of study in a lawyer's
office, doing, in the meantime, a large
amount of labor in the way of drawing
up and copying papers, as was then the
fashion.   When he was at length admitted to the bar, he was, for his first
case, assigned to defend a man who
had been arrested for some misde-
meanor.   Having conferred privately
with the accused, and learning from his
own mouth that he was guilty, Mr.
Temple made but a lame argument in
his defence, and the man was convicted.
The young lawyer was somewhat
abashed, on passing his client immediately after the verdict, to hear him
say to another that his attorney *"did
not plead worth a d—n."*   This remark
set him to thinking.   He had lost his
first case, but justice had been done,
and it was better so.   How could he, as
an honest man, have helped the guilty
to escape?   If his duty as a lawyer required this of him, and it looked to him
as if it did, then, decidedly, the law was

not to his taste. He had a strong and logical mind, and a conscientious desire that the truth might win.

Whether or not these reflections led to a change we do not know, but it is recorded that not long afterwards Mr. Temple was converted during a religious revival which swept over the land, and he determined to study for the ministry. In choosing that profession, he felt that he would be at liberty to follow the truth, lead where it might; so he promptly threw aside the law and entered a theological seminary. But as he progressed in his studies, the same desire for truth which had unfitted him for the practice of the law prevented his following the devious and illogical paths marked out by tradition and taught by his professors. He saw that the Bible required him to lead a sinless life, in full conformity to the divine law, yet no one, not even the professors in the theological school, nor the most eminent clergymen, dared claim that they had attained to that state. Religion was a struggle against sin, with no hope or expectation of really overcoming it.

At length Mr. Temple prepared and read before his society at the seminary an elaborate essay on the question, " Why does not the Christian Church at the present day advance as rapidly as the primitive church did towards the conquest of the world?"   His answer in substance was this:

1. The primitive church freely and earnestly preached the doctrine of perfection; whereas modern churches have fallen back on the 7th chapter of Romans, and are afraid to say anything about perfection.

2. The primitive church took hold on the full strength of God by the prayer of faith; whereas modern churches think that the " age of miracles is past," and, therefore, dare not expect actual and immediate answers to their prayers.

3. The primitive church relied first on personal holiness, secondly on prayer, and thirdly on preaching, as the means of converting the world.   The apostles first yielded themselves wholly to God; then, with their right hand they

laid hold on His strength, while with their left they drew men out of the mire of sin. Whereas the modern churches, reversing the order, rely first on preaching, secondly on prayer, and lastly on personal holiness; and, with little confidence in the efficacy of prayer, lay hold on sinners *with both hands.* Having nothing to support them, it is not strange that instead of pulling sinners out of the mire they are often pulled into it themselves. In conclusion Mr. Temple proposed as a motto, and as a memorial of the order in which the three great subjects ought to stand in people's minds, the words "*Perfection, Prayer, Preaching.*"

This essay caused no disturbance, nor was it regarded as heretical in any degree. But when, led on by a course of reasoning so logical that it was irresistible, Mr. Temple began to teach that men must actually attain to personal holiness if they would be saved, doubts arose as to the soundness of his theology. He himself underwent an inward struggle. He felt that he was trying to save others from sin while he himself was not saved. The pressure of conviction became so great that he withdrew from all public labors, and gave himself up to prayer, searching the scriptures, and striving after full salvation from sin. The law "Thou shalt love the Lord thy God *with all thy heart*" was ever before his mind as the only standard of righteousness, and the very beginning of all virtue. In the blaze of that law all his works and experience and hopes faded into vanity.

Then came the healing and the entering on the upward path that led to salvation. The first step was to have faith, to take God at His word and believe Him implicitly. Then he learned to listen for the voice of God directing him. Sometimes he opened the Bible and read the first verses his eyes fell upon. They bore on the very question he was mentally asking, and he felt that God had answered him. He saw that Christ's resurrection was the central point on which our faith should lay hold, and the necessity of confession as the complement of inward belief was forced upon his mind. He determined at all hazards to at once confess Christ, in himself, a Saviour from sin, believing that God called him to this course and would justify him in it.

Just then it fell to his lot to preach in the evening at a church. He prepared himself during the day for an unflinching testimony against all sin. When he announced from the pulpit his text, "He that committeth sin is of the devil," he felt, and no doubt the congregation felt, that he was entering upon a new field of theology. He insisted upon the literal meaning of the text, and did his best to prove that sinners are not Christians.

The next morning one of the theological students who had heard his discourse the evening before went to labor with Mr. Temple in regard to it. He thought it altogether too stringent, and wished to know if Mr. Temple really meant what he said—that a sinner cannot be a Christian. He was assured that he did so mean. Then came the *ar-*

gumentum ad hominem, "Don't you commit sin?" The answer was given deliberately but firmly "No!"

The man stared as though a thunderbolt had fallen, and rushed away to tell the news. In a few hours the word was passed through the college and the city, "Temple says he is perfect;" and on the heels of this report, "Temple is crazy."

The confession was made, and the consequences came promptly. One of the professors called at Mr. Temple's room to notify him that he was soon to be tried for heresy. He laughed Mr. Temple's confession to scorn, asserting that it is pyhsically impossible for any man to feel the spirit of God. Mr. Temple asked the professor if he did not commit sin? He admitted that he did. Thereupon Mr. Temple repeated the text, "He that committeth sin is of the *devil*."

"You say, then," said the professor, "that I am of the devil, do you?"

"No," replied Mr. Temple; "*you* said you committed sin, and I only quoted the words from the Bible, 'He that committeth sin is of the devil.'"

"Well," said the professor, "you are a sinner now, if you were not when I came in, for you have not treated me courteously."

"In such a case as this," quietly observed Mr. Temple, "the best kind of courtesy is plainness of speech."

The professor left, and Mr. Temple soon resigned his position. He had lost his standing in the church where he had preached, in the ministry, and in the college. His good name in the great world was gone; his friends were fast falling away. He was beginning to be an outcast; yet he rejoiced, because he felt the love of God with him. Someone asked him whether he should continue to preach, now that the clergy had taken away his license. He replied: "I have taken away their license to sin, and they keep on sinning. So, though they have taken away my license to preach, I shall keep on preaching."

While he was going through these deep spiritual struggles, it was Mr.

Temple's habit to read the New Testament through by course, over and over again, each time with his attention on some particular subject. He had broken away from all the old trammels of thought and belief, and had opened his heart to receive the truth in a spirit of simple faith. In reading the Testament thus, he made the momentous discovery that *Christ's Second Coming took place long ago*, within the lifetime of some of His disciples, or about the time of the destruction of Jerusalem. He saw that the churches had for nearly two thousand years been looking in the wrong direction for that event ; that the first judgment has taken place, and that we, who are now on the earth, are living in "the times of the Gentiles."

This discovery greatly strengthened his faith, and he determined that he would hold himself in the attitude of a young convert forever, asking God to lead him and teach him the true way.

CHAPTER III.

THE SPIRITUAL SCHOOL.

For two or three years after breaking away from the churches, Robert Temple led a wandering and uncertain life. His faith grew stronger in the troubles and vicissitudes through which he passed. At length his destined career opened before him. He was to be a social reformer. It is interesting to notice how he was led along, step by step, into his final life-work, without himself knowing whither his course lay. He abandoned himself to the inspiration which came upon him, believing it to be from on high. No one could have had a more earnest and sincere purpose to follow wherever the spirit of truth led. His mind was logical in its action; he cared nothing for the opinions of the world, but thought only how he might please God.

The next we learn of Mr. Temple is

that he returned to his home in an
obscure New England village, where he
married a most estimable young woman
who believed in his doctrines.   Then,
after a time, his mother, his brother,
and two of his sisters became converts
to his views and espoused his cause.
As the years rolled by, others, one by
one, joined him, until he found himself
the leader and teacher of a little group
of families, who had real Christian fellowship together.   Each of these families had its own home, the members
followed their regular avocations, but
all met frequently to read the Bible and
strengthen their faith.

During the course of these meetings
an incident took place which borders
on the marvellous.   After having
prayed together many times, " Thy
Kingdom come, Thy will be done on
earth as it is in Heaven," these believers began to say to themselves that
if they were really saved from sin, and
if they were doing God's will on earth,
then, in truth, that prayer was already
answered.   The Kingdom of God *had*

come on earth. As this thought became impressed on their minds, Mr. Temple arose, and, in solemn, earnest voice, with upturned face, exclaimed, "I confess my belief that the Kingdom of Heaven is come on earth, and that we who believe and have given ourselves wholly to God are now living in it!" The others clasped their hands and cried, "Amen! We also believe!"

Instantly there was a tremendous clap of thunder. It was in the middle of the afternoon. The sun was shining brightly, and those assembled gazed at each other in wonder. Then they ran out of doors to see if a thunderstorm was approaching. Not a cloud was to be seen. The air was still and clear.

Was the thunder a signal of God's approval of their confession? They pondered long and deeply on the incident. The strange sound was never accounted for on any natural grounds, but, in after years, when Mr. Temple and the others used to recount the story, it remained as much a mystery as ever

Several years passed in these peaceful religious studies, during which neither Mr. Temple nor any of his followers had a thought of adopting new social forms. They were intent only on spiritual improvement and the attainment of salvation from sin. But as they progressed in their studies of the Bible they saw that *selfishness* is the great obstacle to spiritual growth. When the Holy Spirit was poured out on the primitive believers on the day of Pentecost, its influence led them to make a common fund of all their money and possessions, and it seemed, from the story of Ananias and Sapphira, that when others joined that early church they were expected to put in all they owned. A deep and earnest purpose was required of all.

Mr. Temple and his friends felt that this was an example for them. They began to study how they might combine their interests more closely. Little by little they found ways of uniting. They contributed to a common fund for publishing a paper which advocated and explained their doctrines. This paper was sent to all who asked for it, no price being put upon it. It was a free gift, and, as after-events showed, the seed thus sown bore good fruit. But the expense of publishing the paper was a heavy tax on their slender incomes. To continue it they established a printing office of their own in one of the dwellings. The women and girls set the type, and the men turned the press by hand. Thus, for nearly ten years, they labored for the cause to which they had given themselves.

It was inevitable that, living as they did, the breath of scandal should assail them. Among those in the neighborhood who became converted to the doctrine of perfect holiness was a young married woman whose husband was an infidel. This woman had been sick eight years, and the physicians were unable to help her. She had been slowly prostrated until, for a year and a half, she was confined to her bed. For six months she was reduced to entire blindness. In the seventh month she

began to see a little, but required the
room to be constantly darkened. Then
she heard of Mr. Temple and became
interested in his teachings. He visited
her, and as she listened to his words
she believed that she could be healed
by faith. This idea took full possession
of her, and when Mr. Temple again
called she said to him that she would
do whatever he bade her. He told her
to sit up in the bed. She did so with
ease.   He then commanded her with
great energy to "Get up," and, taking
her by the hand, he led her to a chair.
Without pain, and with great delight,
she sat before the open window, in the
bright sunlight. Her eyes were now
perfectly well. She gazed about and
drank in the beauty of a world she had
not seen for years. She declared that
she was healed, and she determined to
go home with Mr. Temple that the cure
might be permanent. Her sisters and
a lady friend who was present stripped
off her extra flannels, cap, and "grave
clothes in general," as she calls them in
her narrative, and in ordinary dress she

entered the carriage and rode several miles without fatigue or pain. She was cured.

This wonderful event, being noised abroad, created much jealousy and hostile feeling. The local clergymen declared the pretended healing an imposture. Women are naturally more religious than men, and, in this instance, they were inclined to believe in Mr. Temple. Several of the young and most popular ones joined the new church. This roused the men to a pitch of fury. Many acts of persecution were undertaken, and, at length, Mr. Temple and those who had been most intimately associated with him were driven away from their homes. It looked as if the spiritual school was broken up.

CHAPTER IV.

THE NEW HOME.

In a beautiful and well-watered valley, once occupied by a powerful tribe of Indians, there lived, at the time of which we are writing, an honest farmer and miller named Ephraim Dudley. He was a sober-minded, industrious man, and owned a good, fertile tract of land, on which he had erected a comfortable dwelling and a saw-mill.

By some strange chance copies of the paper published by Mr. Temple had found their way to this secluded spot in another State. Mr. Dudley had read them eagerly, and had become a convert and a regular subscriber. To help on the work, he sent out copies of the paper he had read to good men living near him. In this way two or three other families became interested.

The influence which went out from Mr. Temple had this characteristic—

that it never died out, but constantly
grew and urged men on to the higher
life he taught. Actuated by this influence, Albert and Edward Percival,
and Eugene Hastings soon associated
themselves with Ephraim Dudley in an
effort to establish a common interest on
the gospel basis. Thus several families
were brought together.

This happened just before Mr. Tem
ple and his associates were expelled
from their old home by unbelieving
neighbors. No sooner did Mr. Dudley
and his friends learn of what had happened than they invited Mr. Temple to
make his home with them, offering to
place all they had at his disposal. This
invitation he accepted, and the believers from the spiritual school where
he had taught so many years, soon
rallied around him again. They felt
that their home was where he was. It
became evident to them all that the
breaking up and exile from their former
home was a thing planned and exe-
cuted under the guidance of a friendly
Providence in order that the move-

ment might grow and develop strength.
Their hearts were made glad by the
signs of divine favor which appeared
to encourage them, and they resolved
to build a large unitary home in which
they might all live together. To this
end they organized themselves into an
association which they named "The
Society of the Perfect Life." This
title expressed the object they had before them. They were resolved to live
perfect, sinless, unselfish lives, expecting to be guided thereto by direct inspirations. And they named their loca-
tion "Midvale," as it was the centre of
a beautiful valley.

. A suitable agreement was drawn up
and signed by every member of the
new society. This was called "The
Covenant." In it each agreed, in bind-
ing legal phrase, to give all he or she
possessed to the society, absolutely, and
beyond the power of recall; to abide
by the rules and ordinances of the
society; and to labor without wages or
pay of any kind. In return each member was guaranteed suitable and equal

support, in health and in sickness, and
equal privileges in the common home.
To sign this covenant was to enter the
new life, burning the bridge behind
them. Everyone signed it cheerfully,
putting into the common treasury all
he possessed, and none kept back a
part.

They did not have any formal election of officers. All recognized Mr.
Temple as leader, looking to him for
wisdom to guide them aright. One of
their number was appointed to keep
the books of account, take charge of
the common funds, and make all necessary purchases. He was not required
to give any bonds for the faithful dis-
charge of his duty; no one had a thought
but that he would be faithful. His
books were always open to inspection,
yet no one cared to inspect them. They
were sure to be right.

Almost the first thing Mr. Temple
did after establishing himself in his
new home was to resume the publishing
of a free paper, and this he maintained,
no matter what the other financial needs

might be. The free paper, preaching
the gospel of holiness and advocating
unity and brotherly love, was first in
his estimation. The bread thus cast
upon the waters came back in the
shape of new and substantial members,
who had sold farms, cattle, and crops,
and who brought money in their
pockets, prepared to give all to the
cause.

Among those who joined the society
at this early period were the Stanleys,
the Franklins, the Gregorys, the Ford-
hams, the Morgans, the Millingtons,
the Floyd family, the Pendells and
many other substantial families, besides
single men and women. New members
continued to be received until the society numbered several hundred persons.

In accepting new members, no property qualification was imposed. If an
applicant for membership seemed to
them to have the true faith and purpose he was cordially received, even
though he did not possess a dollar. It
is certain, therefore, that the society
was not organized as a money-making

scheme, else those who had contributed large sums would not have been so ready to share with the poor who wished to join.

In the early years of the associate life these people had no established industries capable of supporting them. They depended on the money brought in by new members, and the treasury was sometimes quite empty. Happily they were never long at a time in severe straits, and it is a noteworthy fact that none of them lost their faith or confidence in such dark times. They kept right along, publishing their free weekly paper as though they had a heavy balance in bank.

During these early years they were forced to exercise the most rigid economy, even in regard to the necessaries of life, but they made light of it. There was no grumbling.

By degrees profitable manufactures were established and the income became ample for their wants. As the society grew in numbers and in wealth, the old buildings were replaced by new and

larger ones of brick. Additional land
was bought until the domain became
sufficiently large. The business and
social organization was, during the same
time, perfected as experience taught the
way, until every part worked in perfect
harmony.

CHAPTER V.

OUT OF THE WORLD.

THE sun was sinking toward the horizon on a bright day in the month of June, when our friend, Mr. Scott, after a ride of several hours by train, arrived at the Society of the Perfect Life, and was installed in comfortable rooms facing the west. His imagination had pictured a large, unitary home, more nearly ideal than any he had ever known; and his heart beat high with the liveliest anticipations. Judged from the glimpses he had caught in a rapid approach, the externals seemed to fully justify his wildest dreams; but these glimpses had only served to stimulate his fancy, and as there was yet a little time before the evening meal would be served, he begged the privilege of taking a hasty walk through the grounds, saying it would refresh him after his ride. Permission being readily granted, he started out by himself.

His course lay through the park which sheltered the mansion on the north. Groups of maples, pines, and other large trees were separated by stretches of smoothly-shaven lawn. Here and there were masses of sweet-scented, flowering shrubs, while in various sheltered nooks rustic seats, fashioned from the limbs of cedar trees cut in a neighboring forest, seemed to entice the weary to an enjoyment of the grateful shade.

Coming at length to the brow of the elevation on which the dwellings were situated, the view broadened. The noble hills on either side of the valley were covered to their tops with forest-trees. Below, well-tilled farms extended to the south as far as the eye could reach, while on the north the hills fell rapidly away until they melted into a broad and level plain. At the bottom of the valley the clear water of a river sparkled in the rays of the setting sun, as it wound its way, with many a turn and tumble, through the meadows and pastures. Herds of well-bred cows and flocks of sheep were grazing near the

bank of the stream, or lying in the cool
shade of the overhanging elms. Groups
of men could be seen here and there
laboring in the fields and vineyards.
At a distance the smoke arising from
several tall chimneys indicated the loca-
tion of the factories owned by the
society.

Turning then to the right, Mr. Scott
obtained a good view of the stately
edifice of brick, trimmed with granite,
which was now to be his home. The
lines of its extended front were so
broken by wings and towers and by the
broad portico which shaded the main
entrance as to create a most pleasing
effect. Flowering Virginia creepers
and other climbing vines had been carefully trained along the walls, while little
beds of pansies, geraniums, and fuchsias
dotted the turf beneath. Although
there were not many people to be seen
about the grounds at that hour, most
of the members being occupied with
their several duties, yet occasional forms
could be seen at the open windows, and
the sound of children's voices came

floating on the air as they played some noisy game.

The delicious, soft atmosphere of early summer shed its charm over this beautiful scene, and it is not surprising that Mr. Scott should have indulged in thoughts of the happiness his new career would yield him. He had left the great, roaring, struggling, selfish world behind him, with its poverty, its misery, and its crimes. Here the external surroundings were such as the imagination would picture for a home where innocence, unselfishness, and loving friendship should banish all strife, jealousy, and selfish competition. Here flowers, cultivated by gentle hands, shed their fragrance for all. Here he would associate only with those who had consecrated their lives to the search for truth, love, and all that is beautiful and good. As he thought of these things, a great sense of peace and rest came over him. He felt himself transported back to the light-heartedness of his boyhood, when he had no care, distrust, or anxiety. The whole atmosphere of the place was reassuring.

Presently the loud blast of a steam-whistle announced the hour when the labors of the day should end and the people prepare for the evening meal. The distant hum of the machinery in the factories ceased; the men in the fields gathered up their implements and started towards the dwelling; the work teams came rattling by on their way to the barns. Mr. Scott retraced his steps, anxious to see the people who had created this Eden, wondering if they would also justify his expectations. He did not look to see finely-dressed gentlemen and ladies of leisure. He knew that the members of the society were sober, industrious workers, that they had toiled early and late to achieve their success. But would he find them genuine of heart and strong of mind and purpose, as he hoped? Would their faith have worked itself out in their daily lives so that they were really saved from sin as they professed? And if so, would their lives be so

austere and forbidding as to crush out
the more delicate human instincts?
He realized how keen would be his
disappointment if the glorious promises
held out here should prove deceptive.
The system established by Father
Temple was unique in the history of the
world; nothing like it had ever before
been attempted. If it succeeded, the
true path to social regeneration would
be opened; if it failed, the world must
struggle on in social darkness for perhaps a hundred years longer, or until
another inspired leader should appear.
How important, then, to see these
people, to associate with them intimately, to study them, and to decide
whether or not he would join them!

Returning to the reception-room, Mr.
Scott found two of the members, a man
and a woman, ready to escort him to
supper.   These were Mr. Pendell and
"Aunt Julia," who were especially assigned to the duty of caring for visitors
and new members. As they entered
the dining-room the tables were being
rapidly filled, promptness at meals be-

ing regarded as a cardinal virtue. The men and women seated themselves haphazard, just as they chanced to arrive. Every one seemed to be perfectly at home with everyone else, so there was not the slightest air of formality. On the contrary, all seemed to be in cheerful, happy mood, chatting and laughing as if they were an immense family of brothers and sisters. One or two tables were reserved for visitors, and here Mr. Scott was seated.

A moment later a man clad simply in black, tall, strongly built, his head grandly proportioned, entered and took a vacant seat near the centre of the room. His hair was beginning to be streaked with silver, and his countenance bore evidence of deep thought. Everything about him betokened power—power of mind and spirit, power of will, power of body. His expression was a wonderful blending of gentleness and severity. It was as easy to imagine him comforting the heartbroken or encouraging those who had been overcome by temptation, as to

behold him assuming the majesty of
spirit and the authority of a leader by
Divine grace.

"That is Father Temple," said Mr.
Pendell.   "Have you met him?"

"No," replied Mr. Scott.   "I have
never seen him before, and you can
imagine what a gratification it is to me,
when I tell you that it is now more
than a year since I first began to read
his writings.   During all that time
something has constantly impelled me
to come here."

"Indeed!   But that has been the
experience of every one of us.   When
the good spirit calls us we must sooner
or later obey."

Mr. Scott was intent on studying
these people.   There was nothing
peculiar in the dress or fashions of the
men, except that few of them shaved.
They wore full beards, trimmed to suit
the individual taste.   There was no
rule about this, but the fashion of wearing beards had come in.   Perhaps it
was more convenient, as it takes time
to shave daily.

What was most surprising was the appearance of the women and girls. These, with the exception of a few elderly women, all had their hair cut short in the neck, and wore short dresses, with pantalettes of the same material. The skirts came a few inches below the knee, and the pantalettes were not gathered at the ankle as in the Turkish costume, but sat jauntily about the foot like a well-cut trouser.

It was surprising to see what a youthful appearance these fashions of dress and of hair gave the women, while the greater freedom and ease of motion which they acquired by escaping from long skirts, added to this effect. Visitors to the society, of whom there were great numbers during the pleasant summer months, attracted partly by curiosity and partly by the beauty of the grounds, often mistook women of thirty and forty years for girls in their teens. These women were bright-looking, rosy-cheeked, and vivacious. If they felt that dread of being peculiar which is common to all their sex, they bravely con-

cealed it, and stood by their principles.
They sought to be healthy and to
crucify mere vanity. No doubt they
were upheld in this by the strong influence of Father Temple, who was glad
to have the line between his people and
"the world" clearly marked.

But aside from fashions of dress and
of hair or beard, there was something
peculiar in the appearance of these
people. It is a well-known fact that the
life a person has led is recorded in his
face. Evil thoughts and the sensual
indulgence of the passions leave their
indisputable marks. This is peculiarly
true of the expression of the eye. The
cold, soulless look in the eye of a gam-
bler or a criminal is easily recognizable.
So, too, good thoughts and the deep
experiences of the soul, which enable the
spirit to subdue and control the passions, leave their marks. From the
eye of a good man or woman a pure,
refined spirit shines forth. Children
are wonderfully quick to recognize these
differences, even where older people
do not detect them. If the expression

of the eye be cold and wicked, no smile
on the lips will deceive a child.

The peculiar expression which was
common to nearly every face in the
Society of the Perfect Life was one of
purity. It begat confidence at once.
Mr. Scott was deeply impressed by it.
He knew, instinctively, that these people
were genuine. He learned afterwards
that this was a characteristic often com-
mented upon. Members who went out
on trips to sell their manufactures would
sometimes, on entering a store they had
never before visited, be welcomed with
some such remark as this:

"Good morning, Member of the Perfect Life, I have never met you before,
but I can recognize one of your people
the instant I set my eyes on him. And
what is more, I am always glad to see
you, because I know you are honest."

CHAPTER VI.

THE EVENING MEETING.

In the Society of the Perfect Life, religion was essentially a matter of the heart, very little importance being attached to external forms or ordinances of any kind, and none whatever to creeds. It was their custom to hold a meeting every evening in the year, from eight o'clock until nine, and this assembling of themselves daily was regarded as a good ordinance. These meetings were not solemn, formal affairs, but were regarded, rather, as family gatherings, the aim being to make them attractive to old and young alike. The children did not attend them, the smaller ones being put to bed at an early hour, while the larger ones were entertained during the meeting hour by two of the adults, a man and a woman, in rotation. This custom was explained to Mr. Scott as the meeting hour approached, so when the whistle sounded again at eight o'clock, he went to the Hall with Mr. Pendell and took his seat with the rest.

This Hall was built in the form of a pretty little theatre, with stage and dressing-rooms, proscenium and curtain, the walls and ceiling being handsomely frescoed. It was capable of seating three or four hundred persons on the floor, while a deep gallery on the sides and back fully doubled its capacity. It was well lighted by lamps hung from the front of the gallery, and was furnished with a piano and an organ. It was, therefore, well adapted for concerts and amateur theatricals, as well as for a chapel and assembly-room. Numerous small hexagonal tables, with additional lamps, gave opportunity for the women to sew or knit during the meeting hour if they felt inclined, and many of them did. This arrangement might be considered in bad taste at a strictly religious meeting, but the aim being to make them sociable and home-like, it was appropriate. It may be remarked, in passing, that the members always spoke of the society as "the family." They all considered themselves as members of the same large household.

When all were seated and the room quiet, a young man arose, and, placing a handful of newspapers on the front of the stage, proceeded to make a condensed report of the news of the day, gleaned from various sources. By practice he had become quite expert in selecting the pithy points, sometimes condensing a whole article into a few sentences of his own, again reading some important matter as printed. Thus, in about fifteen minutes, the whole society had learned all that was necessary to keep them well informed. If anyone desired to go more into detail, he or she could do so afterwards by reading the papers in the library, but the majority found this report sufficient, and it was a great economy of time.

Next, a young woman, advancing to the same position in front of the stage, stood and read such letters as had been

received that day and were of general
interest. A number of these were from
persons who wished to join the society.
Others were from members absent on
business. They were usually spicy and
interesting. Thus another quarter of
an hour was passed, after which the
meeting was open for anyone to speak
who chose. It was in order, after the
reading of the correspondence, to speak
briefly of any business matters which
needed immediate attention.

On this evening Uncle Jonathan
called for a volunteer to milk six cows
night and morning for a few weeks, as
one of the farmers who had this duty
assigned him was not well and needed
rest. Henry Franklin, a powerfully-
built young man, immediately volunteered.

"That's good! I like to see that
prompt and willing spirit of service in
our young men," was Father Temple's
comment.

"I do," said Mr. Gregory. "It shows
that they are growing into the spirit
which built up this society."

"We must study to make labor attractive," added Father Temple. "In a true system, labor is not degrading. It is healthful and ennobling. We must serve one another in the spirit of love and good-will."

These remarks amply repaid Henry for having volunteered to milk, and, in fact, made others wish they had done so. It was evident that in this little world the force of public opinion was great.

Next Aunt Rebecca asked for a "bee" to clean up the lawns, which had become somewhat littered by parties of visitors who had brought their luncheon in baskets and eaten out-of-doors under the trees. This was cordially agreed to, and the time was set for the following evening, after which the chairman spoke as follows:

"We have with us this evening Mr. Alexander Scott, who has come to make trial of our life for a year on probation. I am sure that all will welcome him and try to make him feel at home. If you have anything you would like to say to the family, Mr. Scott, we would be pleased to hear you."

Mr. Scott arose and said: "I thank you for your kind welcome. Being an entire stranger to most of you, and desiring to become acquainted with all, I will frankly state my feelings and objects, so that you may understand me. I have for several years been deeply interested in social questions, seeing the pressing need the world has of better ways of living. But I did not find anything practical which commended itself to my judgment until I came across some of Mr. Temple's writings, quite by accident, in Europe. Since then I have felt a growing interest in your society, which culminated in my asking to be received as a probationary member. I trust that I may be found worthy of your fellowship and confidence. I consider the work you have undertaken to be of the highest importance, and it will be my desire to help it forward, whether I join you permanently or not. I have much to learn about your system, but what I have seen impresses me most favorably."

When Mr. Scott sat down, Father Temple spoke as follows: "I have been well impressed by Mr. Scott's letters, and by his remarks this evening. Acting on my intuitions, I recommend that he be taken into our fellowship. I am always glad to have intelligent people study our system. We have nothing to conceal, but are living for the good of the world as well as for ourselves."

The introduction was evidently considered complete, for the chairman at once said:

"Some of the young people have been invited to entertain us with a little music this evening. Will their manager please come forward and take charge?"

A little space was cleared in front of the piano, and the concert began. It was informal and enjoyable. A vocal quartette, a soprano song by Miss Minette Pendell; a trio by Miss Lily Millington, Miss Emily Floyd, and Mr. George Stanley; then a humorous little recitation by Jennie Lee, and two numbers for violin and piano, by Mr. Hugo

Fairfax with Miss Julia Fordham as accompanist, made up the programme.

The young people of the society were enthusiasts on the subject of music, and although their advantages had been somewhat limited, they were really very good amateur performers. The young men had formed an orchestra of twenty-five pieces, which played in the hall daily, and this being generally known, the hall was often crowded with visitors. Evening concerts were also frequently given, made up of vocal, as well as instrumental, music.

When appearing thus before their little public, the young women still wore the short dress. Minette and Julia were pictures for an artist. Attired in light muslin robes, the only adornment being a little lace at the wrists and throat, they were beautiful. The simplicity of manner of all the girls and the entire absence of affectation clothed them with the charm of vestal virgins. Added to this, their beauty of face and of form, and the real ability with which they sang and played, made them adorable.

Mr. Scott, notwithstanding he had travelled and had seen and heard much, was both surprised and charmed. He had not expected to find any such musical or artistic culture in the society. Father Temple took an evident enjoyment in the music, and when the programme was finished, he proposed that they conclude by all singing the hymn of the society, which he himself had composed at the time when they were about to take possession of their present home. Two hundred voices joined in rendering the following stanzas:

HYMN OF THE PERFECT LIFE.

I.

Let us go, brothers, go,
  To the Eden of heart-love,
Where the fruits of life grow,
  And no death e'er can part love.
Where the pure currents flow
  From all gushing hearts together,
And the wedding of the Lamb
  Is a feast of joy forever—
Let us go, brothers, go.

II.

We will build us a dome
    On our beautiful plantation,
. And we'll all have one home
    And one family relation.
We will battle with the wiles
    Of the dark world of mammon,
And return with the spoils
    To the home of our dear ones—
Let us go, brothers, go.

III.

When the rude winds of wrath
    Idly rave around our dwelling,
And the slanderous breath
    Like the simoon is swelling.
Then so merrily we'll sing
    As the storm blusters o'er us,
Till the very heavens ring
    With our hearts' joyful chorus—
Let us go, brothers, go.

IV.

Now life's sunshine 's begun,
    And the spirit-flowers are blooming;
And the feeling that we're one,
    All our hearts is perfuming.
Toward one home let us all
    Set our faces together,
Where true love shall dwell
    In peace and joy forever—
Let us go, brothers, go.

When the meeting closed, the people did not all disperse at once. Many remained to chat or visit together in little groups of two or three, or more. Mr. Scott heard a gentleman sitting just behind him invite several of the ladies to walk out on the lawn and look at the stars. They assented, and that particular group soon disappeared. In a corner, by another table, an enthusiastic young artist might be seen showing his latest sketches to his friends. The stenographer who had taken notes of the meeting sharpened his pencils afresh, packed up his things, and went away. And so one after another departed.

Father Temple stepped across and shook hands cordially with Mr. Scott, who was then introduced to many of the other members as they came forward. To meet thus face to face the worthies he had thought so much about was a great pleasure. He clasped hands with Mr. Dudley, Mr. Gregory, Mr. Kinglake, Mother Temple, Father Temple's two sisters and his son Mortimer, Aunt Millicent, and half a hundred others, including two of the young ladies who had taken part in the music of the evening, Minette and Julia.

Now it must be told that Mr. Scott had never been in love. Whether it was because his heart had not been ripe for it, or because the fates had held him back, who can tell? But when he first saw Julia he noticed her in a manner unusual to him. She seemed so sweet, so free from artificial ways, so womanly, and so genuine, that he looked at her often. And when he was introduced and clasped her hand he felt something wholly new, something very like a tiny electric shock. I cannot account for this. There comes a time in every man's life when such things happen, unless his soul be dead. Mr. Scott reflected upon it for a long time after his head was on his pillow that night. It was the beginning of a new experience.

CHAPTER VII.

MR. SCOTT FINDS EMPLOYMENT.

Mr. Scott arose early the next morning. He was full of enthusiasm for the new life, and was eager to experience every phase of it as promptly as circumstances would permit. To this end he must in some way take a place in the industrial organization. Fortune favored him. Thinking he would enjoy the cool, clear morning air by taking a turn through the flower-gardens before breakfast, he started out, but had scarcely turned a corner of the dwelling, when he came upon two of the men conversing. As he passed them, he overheard one say to the other.

"I need more help to trim the grapes."

Help was needed, and he wished to begin working. Again approaching the two, he said:

"Pardon me; I overheard you say

you needed help. Could I not be of some assistance in trimming the grape-vines? I know nothing about the business, but presume I could learn."

"You can be of great service just now," replied the elder of the two, who he afterwards learned was Uncle Jonathan, and whose duty it was, for a term, to assign the men to such industrial departments as called most loudly for help. "If you volunteer for the season, I will ask you to join Brother Percival here, as he has charge of the vineyards. The work will not be very heavy, but you must do only so much as your strength will permit. You are not ac-customed to labor, and should begin very gradually."

"Thank you," said Mr. Scott; "I will report to my new officer imme-diately after breakfast," and bowing to Mr. Percival, he continued his walk to the flower-garden.

An hour later, behold Mr. Scott and Mr. Percival in their shirt-sleeves and with broad-brimmed straw-hats on their heads, each armed with a pair of strong shears, each with a bunch of stout twine looped around one suspender, industriously trimming the grape-vines.   In the spring and early summer, especially when the season is wet, the vines make too rapid a growth, unless they are sternly cut back.   Thousands of little, tender shoots and suckers spring out, which must be nipped off so that the juices of the vine may go to develop and mature the fruit; and the shoots which are permitted to grow must be tied to the trellis securely, so that the wind may not break them off.

Some practice is necessary in order to do this work well, and Mr. Scott required to be shown more than once how to select for growth those canes which would make the vine most symmetrical and let in the sunlight to every part.   At length, however, he comprehended the art, and they worked together for several weeks, Mr. Percival on one side of the trellis, Mr. Scott on the other.   During this time they conversed together freely and became very good friends.

If Father Temple had himself chosen a work-fellow for a newcomer, he could not have selected a better one than Edward Percival. He was a thoughtful, scholarly man, and had lived so many years in the society that he was perfectly familiar with its history, its principles, and with the lives of all the members, both before they had joined and since. He was, therefore, able to impart much valuable information, and to make many useful suggestions.

One Monday morning, when they were trimming and tying up the vines as usual, neither having spoken for a little time, Mr. Scott broke the silence.

"In last evening's meeting," he said, "the reader gave us what he called 'The Report of the Business Meeting,' and I was much interested in it. But I did not learn when and where the Business Meeting was held, and thought I would ask you to explain to me fully how the business of the Society is managed. I shall get a clearer idea of it if you will do this than if I pick up the information here and there."

"I will tell you about it with pleasure," replied Mr. Percival. "It is a system peculiar to ourselves, which we have grown into; but it works very well.

"At the beginning of each year we hold a general business meeting in the Hall, which nearly all the men, and as many of the women as choose to do so, attend. At this meeting the profits or losses of each of our departments, as well as the general balance for the past year, are stated; and we then proceed to map out the business for the coming year, and assign individuals to the various industries. First, the general managers are named; one to have charge of the Machine Shops and Foundry; another, the Silk Factory; a third, the Fruit-Canning Factory; a fourth to be Head Farmer; a fifth, Steward; a sixth to take charge of the buildings and grounds, the water-works and drains, and so on.

"As these managers receive no special emoluments of any kind, while they have a much heavier responsibility than those under them, there is no wire-pulling or striving for positions. We all desire to get the best possible returns from our industries, so we calmly select the most capable men to manage them. Thus such appointments are expressions of regard and confidence, and the honor is appreciated. At the same time we think more or less rotation in office is a good thing, as it prevents our getting into ruts, and enables new managers to show their abilities."

"What a contrast to life outside, where every one strives and intrigues for position and authority!" exclaimed Mr. Scott.

"Yes," said Mr. Percival; "by removing the objects for which men ordinarily strive and changing the motives of life wholly, we get rid of much evil. But to continue: when these heads of departments are nominated, they may decline to serve for any good reason, in which case another nomination is made. After the places are filled satisfactorily, the next thing done in this annual business meeting is to assign all the men to suitable posi-

tions under the managers just elected.
In this, much latitude is given to
individual preferences.   Some men
prefer to work outdoors, as we are now
doing; others choose to work in one of
the factories.   Changes are quite frequent; they are easily made, and give
needed variety to prevent labor from
becoming irksome.   Some of the young
men who have musical and artistic
aspirations dislike to do heavy manual
labor, as it would stiffen their fingers
and antagonize their practice.   Take
Hugo Fairfax, for example; he is ambitious to make himself a good violin
player.   He practices hard, and is making good progress.   If he were set to
work digging ditches it would destroy
his fine touch and discourage him, therefore he is given a position as bookkeeper.
Music and art give us much pleasure
and edification, so others who have not
these gifts are quite willing to do the
heavy work."

   "This is very interesting," said Mr.
Scott.   "The world needs a new industrial system which will satisfy all classes

ana all tastes. But is all the business of the year arranged for in this one meeting? I should think exigencies would arise calling for others; or is it left to the managers of departments to carry out the plans then mapped out?"

"No," replied Mr. Percival; "at the annual business meeting we merely decide on a general business policy, elect the managers of departments, assign each his corps of workers, and appoint the standing committees for the year."

"You have not told me about the committees," said Mr. Scott.

"We have a Finance Committee, an Educational Committee, a Subsistence Committee, a Legal Committee, a Traveling Committee, and some others. The Finance Committee has general charge of our finances, assigns a certain amount of capital to each productive department, giving most to those departments which earn most, and appropriates what it deems wise to the expense departments, such as subsistence, laundry, traveling for pleasure,

etc. The Traveling Committee man-
ages the sum appropriated for pleasure
traveling so that each member who
desires to visit his relatives or go else-
where shall have a fair and equitable
share of it. The Legal Committee
looks after all contracts, transfers of
real estate, difficult collections, and like
matters, one principal duty being to
keep us out of lawsuits. This will give
you an idea of the committees."

" Does it never happen that persons
are dissatisfied with the decisions of the
committees?" asked Mr. Scott. "In
the matter of traveling, for example,
suppose a member asked for money to
make a journey and the committee did
not allow it, what would happen then?"

" The committee would have nothing
to gain or lose by withholding money
in such a case. If they refused, it
would be because the fund was ex-
hausted for that year, or because, in
their opinion, the member was trying
to do more than his fair share of the
traveling. In either case public opinion would sustain the committee. The

next year a new committee would be appointed and a new appropriation made. Then the member could try again."

"I see. And as no one could have a personal motive in refusing him, the chances are that justice would be done."

"Exactly so. But I have not yet told you about the business meeting of which you heard the report read last evening. In addition to the annual meeting I have described, we hold a meeting every Sunday morning at eleven o'clock, in which any member is at liberty to bring up any subject, make any proposition, or ask for a special appropriation of money for any particular purpose. The women frequently ask to have new conveniences provided, closets enlarged, walks repaired, more horses and carriages for their use, and things of that sort. If they carry this too far, the men get up an enthusiasm for retrenchment and economy, which counterbalances it. In these meetings a woman's vote counts for as much as a man's; but we aim at securing sub-

stantial unity in everything, and if a
large minority should dissent from any
proposed action, it would be apt to be
deferred until we could all see it alike.
I do not remember that we have ever
lost anything by this course, but I do
know we have avoided troubles which
we would have rushed into if we had
allowed a bare majority to go ahead."

"That is certainly a new principle,"
said Mr. Scott. "Substantial unity
must be a very good rule if it does not
give a chance for some contrary one to
try to have his way by opposing the
will of the majority, while he claimed
that no action should be taken until all
were agreed. By holding out he could
set his will above all the rest."

"We prevent that in this way: a
record is kept of all the transactions in
the business meetings, and this is read
to the whole family in the Sunday
evening meeting. Then any one who
was not at the business meeting, and
who thinks a mistake has been made,
has an opportunity to object and re-
open the matter. A vote in the even-

ing meeting would either confirm or reverse a decision of the business meeting, because more members would be present. Finally, nothing is done without Father Temple's sanction and approval. So if any egotistical obstructionist should arise, public attention would be called to him, and he would soon feel an inclination to sit down again."

"How did you happen to select Sunday forenoon for these meetings?"

"Because we are then at leisure to attend. On other days we are dispersed to our several duties."

"I have noticed that you do not observe Sunday as a day of worship."

"No, we take it as a day of rest, but do not have any legality about it. We feel it our duty to serve God every day in the week, and we cannot do more on Sunday."

"That is quite true, but the Churches will be apt to find fault with your system in that respect."

"Undoubtedly; the Jews found fault with our Savior because He did things

on the Sabbath which their laws did
not allow. Christ brought in a new
dispensation—that of grace instead of
law. He pointed out clearly that to do
good is the main thing. The Churches
are prone to rely on forms and days,
instead of on grace and inspiration.
That is why they do not progress as
they should."

"This brings us naturally to the
question of spiritual and social leadership," said Mr. Scott. "Does Father
Temple choose his assistants in these
higher departments, or are they
elected?"

"Men and women grow into such
positions as they are fitted for," replied
Mr. Percival. "Certain ones of our
number who are most spiritually minded
naturally have most influence. They
are not elected, nor are they appointed
in any formal way. They begin to
exercise certain functions in giving
advice and administering necessary criticism, and if they do it in a good spirit,
so as to create love instead of ill-feeling,
they come to be recognized after a time

as having a share of authority. If, on the contrary, they should exhibit a bad spirit, their authority and influence would come to an end."

"And I suppose spiritual-mindedness is a thing of cultivation and growth, is it not?" asked Mr. Scott.

"Just so. All true religious experience is progressive. At first, in childhood and youth, our natural appetites and desires rule us, but, as we get older and are converted, little by little the spirit triumphs over the flesh. When one arrives at a point in his experience where he no longer gives way to temptations in any instance, he may fairly claim to be spiritually minded. We hope that every member of our Society is progressing in this way. It is certain that a constant struggle is going on. Every one is, or should be, making an earnest effort to attain to that state. Our leaders have much to do in helping those who are weak and those who stumble or fall. Mother Temple is like a visiting angel to those who get into trouble. She has a gentle disposition, and encourages and comforts every one. Yet she is a very earnest woman."

"Yes; I have spoken with her. She seems a very lovable and true-hearted woman. By the way, you did not tell me whether the women of the Society have a business organization corresponding to that of the men? Do they also elect officers and appoint each one a corps of assistants?"

"Their organization is much the same; they hold meetings of their own, elect a Stewardess, a Chief Housekeeper, a Mother of the Children's House, a Buyer, and so on. Women seem to like frequent changes in labor, so they appoint two of the young women to recast their duties every week. These two have a deal of running about to consult every one and get her consent to take a place which must be filled."

"I gather from your statement of the business organization that most of your practical affairs are decided by the vote of the members, men and women voting alike. This is more democratic than I had supposed."

"That is true," said Mr. Percival. " If certain individuals have more influence than others, it is because they have shown their good judgment and wisdom in a way to win the confidence of the others and so get their views adopted. If they were to make serious mistakes, they would no longer be followed. We go by the results."

Here the whistle sounded for dinner, and the conversation ended.

CHAPTER VIII.

SOCIAL FORCES.

As Mr. Scott became more settled in his new home he was much impressed with the feeling of *enthusiasm* which seemed to pervade the whole society. Whatever was to be done, whether in work, study or play, was gone at with a vim, a will, and a boundles good-nature quite surprising in people who had no private or individual gain in view. He observed that this trait was common to all, old and young, men and women, and he did not at first under-stand its cause. It was merely the result of living in such a large family, where each member had so many friends and acquaintances, and where each strove to make others happy.

There is a natural magnetic attrac-tion between men and women which is, under true conditions, as certain and constant and powerful in its action as that of the electric current in a well-designed motor. Its influence is able to transform labor into play, lighten hardship and suffering, and lead one to do cheerfully what would, without it, be very irksome. It is natural to every man to enjoy the companionship of pleasant, wholesome women; and it is natural to every woman to enjoy the companionship of pleasant, wholesome men, even when they are not in love with each other.

In ordinary society, where each family lives by itself, this feeling can only be indulged by arranging parties and balls at which people may, for a little time, associate with others than the members of their own family. At the best they can get only a slight taste of the pleasure there is in such wider association, before they are obliged to return to their old isolated routine.

In the Society of the Perfect Life, all the members lived in the enjoyment of such wide association as their habitual state, and it was largely this which gave them the feelings of enthusiasm and

courage which so impressed Mr. Scott.
Here everything was arranged with a
view to making the natural magnetic
attraction between men and women
work for good ends.   Father Temple
planned to have the sexes associate as
much as possible in labor, in recreation,
and in studies.   The men helped the
women in the in-door work, and the
women helped the men in the out-door
work, not regularly nor all the day, but
in "bees," and in such ways as were
attractive.   The men and women, the
boys and girls, mingled freely in all the
activities of life—and the society was
large enough to give the variety of
companionship which is necessary to
the highest happiness.   Thus the feelings were kept always fresh and strong,
and the enthusiasm was boundless.

In a word, every member of the
society was in a state of perpetual
courtship; not a courtship of one man
and one woman, but of a hundred men
and a hundred women, each giving
such attention to all the others as
circumstances drew forth.   The beauty

of it was that there were no reactions. The enthusiasm, the courtship, and the general love kept up. This made it possible for the members to submit to necessary regulations and to discipline which sometimes cut severely into the natural man. Next to the religious afflatus, it was the bond which held the society together.

In the early days of the society, when they had no hired help, but did all their own work, including even the most menial service, it was the custom to introduce a spice of chance in the organizing. Printed cards bearing the names of all the men were put in one box, blank side up, and the names of all the women in another box, then a man and a woman drew out these names haphazard, while a secretary wrote them down. The washing, hanging out clothes, waiting at table, washing dishes, setting the tables in the dining-room, and other such duties, were provided for in this unique way. A list was made out and read in the Sunday evening meeting. It will be seen that the men and women were drawn in couples, by chance, for doing these duties together for the space of a week. Those whose names were drawn for washing the clothes were called at four o'clock in the morning, so as to get a good start. They worked until seven o'clock, when the couples ate breakfast together, and were then relieved by another set of workers, who finished early in the afternoon. It was surprising how the huge wash was thus disposed of by a unitary effort in which both sexes engaged. The magnetic feeling we have described helped in all such ways.

It will be readily admitted that while no one might really enjoy being called at four o'clock for such service, yet to have a sweet woman for a partner, and perhaps one whom you had not previously known well, to have her pin on your apron, to chat with her, to help her by giving her all the easy pieces, and, finally, to take her in to breakfast in a perfectly familiar, friendly way, was a mitigating circumstance which went far to reconcile one to stern, unavoidable duty-doing. That much may certainly be claimed for the system.

Some part of this old custom was yet retained at the period when Mr. Scott joined the society, although the washing was now done by a regular laundry force, aided by improved machinery. Names of men were still drawn for milking the cows, the term of service being six months; and it happened that one Sunday evening, at the time of which we are writing, the reader announced in evening meeting the names of Philander Koote and George Stanley to milk, as successors to Mr. Kinglake and Arthur Dudley, whose term had expired. It was etiquette to accept all such appointments cheerfully, but on this occasion Philander Koote spoke up as follows:

"I would like to be excused from taking my turn in the milking. Those who milk have to rise at five o'clock every morning, and I find that such early rising injures the flow of my inspiration, so that I am not able to

write for our paper as forcibly as I other
wise would. It seems to me that our
young men should have a spirit of
service such as would make them ready
to volunteer to do all the milking. I
was very much pleased with Henry
Franklin's spirit about milking when
he volunteered some time ago. Perhaps some other young man will now
volunteer to take my place."

There was silence. No one volunteered. The sad truth was that Philander was an extremely lazy man, and
everybody knew it. In this particular
he was in a class by himself. He was
large of frame, strong as a moose, but
wofully lacking in energy. When he
walked, he dragged his long limbs after
him in a weary way, and as he wore
enormous, square-toed boots, built on
a reform last of his own devising, the
effect was quite distressing. Mr.
Koote's indolence had been a sore trial
to the Society, so dependent was it on
the industry of its members. His
example was exceedingly bad, and the
young men had more than once been

on the point of open rebellion at his shirking ways. They would probably have put up with it patiently enough as an infirmity of disposition, but unfortunately, Mr. Koote was ambitious of spiritual influence and authority in the little church. His pretentions to high spiritual attainments made it very hard to endure his laziness.

So now no one volunteered to take his place in the milking. The silence became embarrassing.

Several of the young men might have been seen to smile. George Stanley even winked at Henry Franklin. Evidently they enjoyed the situation and were going to stand out.

Suddenly Mr. Millington volunteered. He was a man beyond middle life, and his action was in effect a rebuke to the young men. They evidently felt it to be so, for Henry Franklin now spoke up:

"I guess there would have been plenty of volunteers if we had not been puzzling over what Mr. Koote said about his inspiration being impaired by

milking.   We young men are all ambitious of becoming inspired, and if milking stops it in Mr. Koote, it would be
apt to delay it in us, so we hesitate.
If that is a fact, which Mr. Koote
alleges, it follows that ·we must either
go without milk, or always keep a
certain uninspired set to get up in the
morning and do the chores."

There was logic in this, and poor
Philander began to get very red in the
face.   What could be done if the
young people were going to openly
scoff at his claims to inspiration in this
way?   He felt that the situation was
serious.   Hard labor stared him in the
face.   But Father Temple spoke :

"We should all cultivate a love of
service.   Sometimes men who work hard
every day are lazy in spirit.   They labor
because they must, but dislike to do it,
and would be very glad if they could
shift their burden upon others and lead
a life of ease and indolence themselves.   But inaction is not always rest.
Sometimes intense activity relieves us.
A young man who has been hoeing

corn all day under a hot sun will take a
long walk with the girls in the evening
rather than lie down to rest. Notice
the boys; be they ever so tired, they
will start off on a run to dig bait and
go fishing! So exertion is rest when
our heart is in it, and if we can once
realize how much good we are doing to
others by such service as milking, it
will not seem irksome. It all depends
on what is our object in life, and the
way we look at things."

Then Robert Dunton spoke: " I will
ask Mr. Millington's permission to
volunteer in his stead, being a younger
and stronger man. Putting it as
Father Temple does, I shall be glad to
milk, but I did not see exactly how I
could do it on Mr. Koote's plan. I can
see the justice of what Father Temple
says about laziness."

Father Temple: " The best way to
treat a lazy person will be to drop him
out of the industrial organization. Let
him go entirely free without doing anything, and, my word for it, he will tire
of it before you will, even though you

should have to do his share in the
meantime. We all respect those who
have willing hearts and hands, but not
the indolent. Still, we must remember
that brain labor counts as well as manual
labor. If a man can write well, he may
be doing more good than another who
works hard with his hands."

Here the clock struck nine, and the
meeting closed. Mr. Scott had been
greatly interested in the incident we
have described. It revealed to him an
entirely new way of treating faults of
character. Instead of hastening to
make such rules as would compel a lazy
member to work, Father Temple aimed
to correct the disposition, or tone up
the spirit, so that the person would go
to work cheerfully and of his own free
will. It was governing by grace and
love, instead of by legality. Mr. Scott
could not help wondering, however,
whether such mild treatment would
effect a cure in an individual so self-
complacent as Mr. Koote appeared to
be. It will be seen, later, that sterner
treatment did become necessary, and
was faithfully applied.

CHAPTER IX.

A MODEL EXCURSION.

One evening in the latter part of June, the chairman of the meeting announced that a large excursion party from a city lying to the north was coming on the morrow to visit the society. It was an influential church organization, with many of their outside friends. The pastor wrote that nearly a thousand tickets had already been sold for the special trains, and that undoubtedly the final number would be much larger. Nearly half of them wished dinner served on their arrival. The rest would bring baskets, and would picnic on the grounds.

Such excursions to the society were of frequent occurrence in the summer time. A railway which ran through their land had a convenient station just in the rear of the dwellings. Visitors by train could therefore alight on the grounds of the society, and as these were extensive enough to accommodate an unlimited number and were well shaded, it was a favorite resort.

To furnish food and entertainment to so large a party involved much labor. Nearly every member was drafted into the service, a list of appointments being read in the evening meeting. The men and women were paired off in all this labor, according to their custom. The force assigned to the duty of serving ice cream and other light refreshments to the excursionists, included the following names:

George Stanley, Mr. Scott, Robert Dunton, Mrs. Gregory, Julia Fordham, and Lily Millington.

Mr. Scott was pleased to hear his name included with the others. It was the first time it had been done, and it seemed to him to indicate a feeling of growing confidence. He was also pleased to hear Julia's name read in connection with his own, but was puzzled to account for it. Was it a lucky turn of chance or a friendly Providence? or had he in some unguarded moment, by act or look, betrayed the interest he felt in her? He had intended to keep his secret most carefully, as he was only a probationary member and was very doubtful how his attentions might be received. But, however the arrangement might have come about, he resolved to make the most of his opportunities, in the way of getting better acquainted with her. He had not yet spoken to her, except when they were first introduced in the Hall, but he had seen her almost daily, and with increasing interest.

The next morning every one was astir bright and early. All signs pointed to a perfect day, and these people knew by experience that other parties than the one announced were likely to arrive. So large preparations must be made. Many bushels of strawberries and green peas must be picked, and a general "bee" had been called to do this before breakfast.

Mr. Scott arose at five o'clock, and after a hasty toilet started off for the

strawberry field.   He had not gone far
when he overtook two of the girls,
Julia and Lily, who were also on their
way to the field.   Here was another
friendly coincidence.   Fortune was
evidently determined to favor him that
day.   Why not pick strawberries with
Julia and so prepare himself for serving
ice cream with her?   Coming up with
the girls he said:

"Good-morning, ladies; I suppose
you are, like myself, marching to the
field of battle.   Shall we travel the rest
of the way together?"

"With pleasure," replied Julia.   Then
she asked: "Have you attended any of
our strawberry bees?"

"No," he said, "I have not, and I
fear I may not be of much service now.
I have not picked strawberries since I
was a little boy and used to hunt for
wild ones to fill a tin cup I carried.
That was a long time ago."

"You will find this quite different,"
said Lily.   "If you are not used to it I
guess it will make your back ache."

"I shall not mind if it does," he

replied. "Working in such pleasant company will overcome any little difficulties."

"I am not so sure of that," said Julia, laughing. "Wait until you have tried it; then you may think differently."

With this they arrived at the berry-field, where an attendant furnished them baskets and directed them where to commence. The beds of vines were separated by narrow walks which were well mulched with clean straw, and were just wide enough for two persons, working opposite each other, to pick across comfortably.

The vines were loaded with luscious, ripe fruit. A quart or two could frequently he picked without moving from one's position, and some of the boys and girls who were very active sometimes picked as many as a hundred quarts each in a day. With such a yield it did not take a very long time to procure all that were needed. Mr. Scott conversed quietly with Julia, and became more and more—what shall I say?—charmed, every minute. He said to himself that a woman who was so wholly attractive and lovable when dressed plainly in calico, working in the bright sun, without a single illusion or artificial aid, who was so gentle and cheerful and altogether sweet, was worthy of any man's admiration and love.   He felt his heart go out to her, and he determined to try to win her love in return.   He could hardly realize that an hour had passed when it was announced that the "bee" was over, and everyone rose to return.

It was nearly noon when the special train, which was run in two sections, each drawn by two locomotives, rolled into the station, one section after the other, and emptied its unusual load. The conductors stated that they had brought, in all, fifteen hundred passengers.   Many of these people had visited the Society before, and having their favorite retreats under the trees, now made haste to occupy them.   The picnic parties opened their baskets and spread out goodly arrays of eatables.   A large swing at the north side of the lawn was put to immediate service. The croquet grounds and tennis courts were also filled with players, eager to enjoy themselves. Those men who had bespoken dinner now went to the office to buy their tickets, while their ladies made themselves smart after their ride on the train.

One stalwart young man, whose appearance would indicate that he was a tiller of the soil, seemed to have some misgivings about buying his tickets. He had just read a notice which was posted conspicuously beside the cashier's window, to the effect that neither tea, coffee, nor meat of any kind would be served at meals, but that an abundance of good vegetables and fruits could be depended upon. The price of the tickets was one dollar each. To pay two dollars merely to dine himself and his girl seemed to him a serious matter.

"No tea, coffee, nor no meat," he said as he advanced to the window. "What do you have that is filling? It can't be you charge a dollar just for vegetables?"

"Buy your tickets, eat your dinner, and if you are not entirely satisfied come back here and I will refund your money," said the cashier.

As the young giant was already experiencing the pangs of hunger, and those on the line behind him began to grumble at the delay he was causing, this assurance decided him and he bought the tickets.

About two hours afterwards he re-appeared in the office, his countenance suffused to almost a purple hue, radiant with smiles and laughter. Thrusting out a large hand to be shaken by the cashier, he shouted:

"My friend, that was the best dinner I ever ate in my life! Keep the two dollars; you are welcome to them. You didn't make a cent on me, not a red cent, by George!" and with that he smote his huge thigh with his right hand so that it cracked like a pistol, and strolled out upon the grounds, happy and contented.

To eat a dinner at the Society was an event to be remembered. It is true,

they served neither tea, coffee, nor
meat at the period of which we are
writing, but, once seated at the table,
the absence of these was forgotten.
The potatoes warmed in fresh, sweet
cream delicately seasoned, the peas,
tomatoes, and nearly every vegetable
at its best, the omelettes made as only
Aunt Margaret could make them, the
excellent home-made bread of which
visitors could never eat enough, the
strawberries and cream, the ice-cream,
cakes, lemonade and chocolate, and,
last but best of all, the wonderful strawberry shortcakes, left nothing to be
desired. The peculiar charm of these
dinners was in their delicacy and fine
quality. The fruits and vegetables
were brought in fresh from the vines,
the cream and butter fresh from the
dairy; and the cooking itself was so
delicate that the exquisite flavor of the
dishes was a revelation to those city
people who were forced to buy all their
fruits and vegetables in a more or less
wilted condition. The difference was
like that which one experiences between

eating a trout which has been exposed
in a city market after a long journey by
rail, and one which has just been pulled
from a cool mountain brook; or like
the difference between oysters eaten in
Baltimore and in Kansas.

After nearly five hundred people had
eaten one of these memorable dinners,
a concert was given in the Hall. No
charge was made for the concerts, nor ·
for the use of the grounds, but only for
meals and refreshments. The orchestra
played several pieces; there were songs,
and a very pleasing little pantomime
performed by the children in costume
on the stage. The pressure for admis-
sion was so great that after the programme had been gone through, the
Hall was cleared and filled again by an
entirely fresh audience, when the concert was repeated.

Meantime the visitors had been avail-
ing themselves of opportunities to get
information which would be useful to
them. Farmers went in groups to look
at the barns and the improved breeds
of cattle and sheep which the Society

kept. Often purchases were made of animals for breeding. Those interested in fruit-growing wandered through the orchards and vineyards, making inquiries as to the best varieties and noting methods of cultivation. The women spent much time in the flower-gardens, and did not neglect a visit to the kitchen to get certain recipes for cooking. Several large omnibuses were kept plying between the dwelling and the silk factory, carrying loads of the visitors who were curious to see how silks are made. In like manner the fruit-canning establishment was constantly overrun by people interested in witnessing the processes.

When at length the hour for the departure of the excursion trains drew near, and all were assembling at the station, many of the members went out to bid them good-bye. It had been a most enjoyable day. Nothing had occurred to mar their pleasure, and every-one seemed to be in happy mood. Mr. Scott and his little corps of workers went out with the others to witness the start.

Father Temple always took a great interest in such events, and he was now standing on a grassy knoll overlooking the station and the trains, when the pastor of the visiting Church, accompanied by several ladies, approached him.

"Father Temple," said the pastor as he took his hand, "we want to tell you how much we enjoy coming here. We have had a peaceful, happy day of pure enjoyment. There has been no drunkenness, no gambling, no fighting, such as occur at almost every other holiday resort. The ladies appreciate this freedom from revolting sights, and in the name of my people I thank you for your hospitality."

It happened that Father Temple was suffering from a sore throat, so he excused himself from speaking, merely acknowledging the friendly expressions of the other.

"You do not need to speak," said the worthy pastor. "*Your works speak for you.*"

Mr. Scott heard these remarks, and

could not help wishing that the Rev. Mr. Langford had heard them too.

But what of our friend Scott? How had he passed the day? He had experienced something quite unexpected. Engaging in his duties with the greatest enthusiasm, full of admiration of Julia, it was not long before he discovered that George Stanley also felt a very tender regard for her. He detected George in various little acts and looks of gallantry, and the way Julia treated him led him to believe that the relation between the two was tolerably well-established. This gave him quite a shock, but he had sufficient control of himself to conceal his feelings. He became more sober and reserved, however, in spite of himself, and Julia, with a woman's quick sense, noticed this. She thereupon took pains to chat with him, and finally succeeded in thawing him out again. She was his partner for the day, so it would have been wrong to neglect him. Perhaps she had a deeper motive. Was she becoming aware of Mr. Scott's state of heart?

CHAPTER X.

Mr. Scott was a man of unexceptionable habits as the world goes, yet he soon found that he could not enter a society like this of the Perfect Life without undergoing some inward struggles. The first trial he encountered was in regard to tobacco. He was a confirmed smoker, and had laid in several boxes of his favorite brand of cigars before starting for the Society. On arriving, he had found that none of the members used tobacco in any form. He scarcely knew what to do with his cigars, but concluded to smoke them up in a quiet way without making them conspicuous or offensive, and resolved that when they were gone he would make an heroic effort to break off the habit.

Only a few cigars now remained. He used them more and more sparingly until, at length, he deliberately smoked the last one and threw aside the empty box. Then came the abstinence, the craving, the gnawings of the appetite, which every smoker who has ever tried to break off will understand. The struggle actually made him feverish and ill. One evening when he felt particularly low-spirited from this cause, he wandered out on the lawn, seeking a secluded nook. As he picked his way through a clump of shrubbery he came suddenly upon Father Temple seated alone, and would have retreated; but the leader asked him to sit down, saying he wished to speak with him.

"It has seemed to me that you are unhappy of late," he said. "If I can be of any service to you in the way of counsel, or in removing any difficulties you may have encountered in your experience here, I shall be glad to help you."

"I should be pleased to become better acquainted with you," said Mr. Scott, seating himself, "but I ought not to put any of my troubles upon you who have so many cares and responsibilities. My main difficulty just at present may seem to you a laughable one, caused by my trying to leave off the use of tobacco. I have smoked considerably for many years, and the habit has obtained a firmer hold upon me than I supposed. I would not have believed it could be so difficult to leave off. I smoked my last cigar some days ago, and have been having serious times ever since."

"I have been through that experience myself," said Father Temple, smiling, "and know just how dreadful it is. I very well remember once making a great resolution to leave off chewing, and I threw away a half-used plug of tobacco into the grass where I was sitting. After a time the craving for it became so severe that I went back to try and find it but could not."

At this both men laughed heartily.

"I am suffering from that terrible craving for a cigar," said Mr. Scott. "How did you finally overcome it?"

"I could not fully break up the habit

until after we assembled here. Nearly all our men used tobacco in some form. It was our custom to buy a large can of fine-cut and keep it in the kitchen, so that everyone of us could go and fill his box daily. But we came to see what a disagreeable, filthy habit it is, and how much pleasanter our home would be without the smoke, the spittoons, and the expectorating. I think the women at length rose up and challenged us to leave it off. At any rate the matter was discussed in our evening meetings and we finally voted to all quit it together, beginning on a certain day. There was some groaning and lamenting, but on the whole we found it quite easy, doing it together in that unitary way. At all events we got our freedom from bondage to the tobacco principality, and have kept it. I hope you will persevere and overcome it too. Can you not take up some new enterprise to distract your attention until the craving passes away?"

"I have not thought of any, but perhaps I might. I find myself feeling

rather low-spirited. A sense of loneli-
ness comes over me at times. All
your people seem to have a deep heart-
acquaintance with each other, very
different from anything I have ever
known before. Perhaps this makes me
feel my own situation by contrast."

"Have you ever had any good,
bright religious experience?" asked
Father Temple.

"Nothing beyond ordinary church
experience. I was brought up to
believe in God, and have attended
church quite regularly, but not always
of the same denomination."

"They are mostly dead," said Father
Temple. "They do not pretend to be
able to save their members from sin,
and they will not accept the truth
about Christ's Second Coming. I had
to leave them and found a church of my
own."

"Yes, I have read your early history
and, in fact, most of your published
works," said Mr. Scott. "The logical
force of your reasoning made a convert
of me long before I ever met you."

"That is interesting. But to return
to your experience: I think you will,
after a little, learn to avail yourself of
such victories as we have won over the
tobacco principality. As you get more
into the current of our life this will be
easy. The first thing is to try and get
a better acquaintance with God. We
should every one of us feel that He is
our personal friend, leading us and guid-
ing us continually. You must ask Him
to help you and to lead you into new
and brighter experience. Believe that
He will do it and you will find it coming
right along. Very likely it may not
take the form you would expect, but it
will be what is best for you. I live by
practical faith of that kind."

"That is precisely what I should be
glad to do. Your words are precious to
.me, and I will endeavor to take them
into my life. I cannot thank you too
heartily for your kind interest."

"After your heart becomes warm and
tender towards God," continued Father
Temple, "He will give you a true love
for woman, and you will find your life

open to all the higher and more enobling influences. The love and fellowship which come to you in that order, the love of God taking the lead, will seem to you like gifts from Him. They will be a blessing to you and all concerned. It is now time for the evening meeting, and we must go in. I hope you will take part in our meetings. Speak out what is in your heart. That will break the ice and start you into the current. And come to me at any time when I can be of use to you."

Mr. Scott hardly knew how to construe Father Temple's remarks about the love of woman. Was it a sequence of logical thought, intended to convey the idea that when once the heart is established in the love of God, a true love of woman will naturally follow? or was it a delicate suggestion that Mr. Scott should avoid any social attachments until such time as his spiritual attainments would warrant them? He pondered on this and resolved to take heed to his steps.

CHAPTER XI.

COMPLEX LOVE.

In the succeeding days Mr. Scott
found his affairs becoming more compli-
cated. Notwithstanding he tried to
take heed to his steps, he was aware
that he was getting deeply in love with
Julia Fordham, and he was uncertain
how such an attachment would be
looked upon by the leaders of the
society. It might be considered quite
out of order for a probationary member
to be indulging in such sentiments
towards a full member. He was not
even certain that Julia herself would
look upon his attachment with favor,
though her manner in their ordinary
intercourse was friendly and pleasant.
He had not yet ventured to speak to
her about his love, but was feeling his
way cautiously. And now he had
discovered that George Stanley was
also an admirer of Julia, and as he was

a handsome, smart young fellow, this knowledge was not altogether reassuring. It was Mr. Scott's first love affair. He was ordinarily a calm, self-possessed sort of man, but his feelings were now agitated by hopes and fears, and by a wish that George Stanley would by some chance become interested in another girl. In vain he said to himself, over and over again, that George was first on the field, and that he himself had no rights. He could not restore his serenity by any such reasoning.

George was, if Mr. Scott had only known it, quite as much disturbed on his part. To be sure, he had youth in his favor, but Mr. Scott was every inch a gentleman, and had the advantage of the refinement of manner which come with travel and much contact with men. So George feared he might be supplanted in Julia's affections, and he groaned in spirit when he thought of it.

Driven on by such feelings, each of these men became very attentive to Julia, and she, being a bright girl, was soon aware of their state of mind. It was unpleasant to her to be thus contended for. Special, exclusive love attachments were not favored in the society, as they were found to bring in jealousies and selfish claims. Julia was aware of this, and the situation at last became so trying to her that she resolved to take counsel of Father Temple in regard to it. Whenever any of the young people found themselves getting into perplexities they always went to Father Temple for help. He was ready to give advice, and criticism if need be. After hearing Julia's statement of her situation, in which she appealed to him to help her out of the embarrassment of it, he took time to consider it well, and then advised George Stanley to offer himself for criticism.

It must be known that in the Society of the Perfect Life they had what was called a system of " Mutual Criticism," which consisted in the practice of telling one another their faults in the spirit of love and good will. This might be difficult, if not wholly impossible, should two persons endeavor to confer such a benefit on each other at the same time. It would inevitably lead to controversy. The system, as practised in the society, was this:

When a person found himself, or herself, suffering from temptation, or not able to hold himself in the clear spiritual atmosphere which he desired, he would offer himself for criticism. If trouble was seen to be gathering which threatened the peace of the society, and the individual involved did not of his own accord ask for criticism, some friend, or one of the leaders, would suggest to him the benefit he might derive from one, as Father Temple had now suggested to George Stanley. Then a number of persons capable of giving good advice would be called together as a committee, the one desiring the benefit meeting with them. One by one they would faithfully tell him his faults of character, and even discuss his conduct in detail with the utmost frankness. It was understood

that the person criticised should sit
silent and thoughtful, listening to all
that might be said without making any
reply or seeking to justify himself in
any way. This was sometimes hard to
do, because others see our characters
and conduct in quite a different light
from ourselves, and we long to show
them how mistaken they are.

When Burns wrote his famous lines:

> O wuid some power the giftie gie us,
> To see oursel's as ithers see us,

he had not heard of mutual criticism.
If he had he would have written a royal
verse in praise of it, for this is just what
such criticisms did. They enabled
everyone to see themselves as others
saw them.

As Julia had mentioned Mr. Scott in
her talk with Father Temple, he also
was invited to be present, the place and
hour being mentioned. Promptly at
the appointed time he made his way to
the South Sitting-Room, where he
found some twenty persons, men and
women, including Julia, already assem-

bled.   Presently Father Temple entered
and took an arm-chair which had been
reserved for him.   After a short pause,
in which he sat with his eyes closed and
arms folded, apparently in meditation
or in prayer, he introduced the subject
thus.

"Julia Fordham came to me a day or
two ago to tell me some of her experience and to ask my advice.   She was in
some worry of mind over her love affairs,
and as she felt that George Stanley was
getting into a wrong, claiming attitude
towards her, I advised George to offer
himself for criticism, which he has now
done.   I judge that so far as George is
concerned this has become a case of
selfish, special love, calling for attention.   I do not wish to condemn George
for loving Julia.   That is quite natural,
but it is very important that such matters
should be managed so as not to let in
false, evil tendencies; and it seemed to
me best to call together those most
directly concerned and have a frank,
sincere talk about it.   As Mr. Scott is
perhaps not fully informed in regard to

our social theories and practices, I have invited him to meet with us.

"We must keep clearly in mind the radical difference between our system and that of the world. In no other department is this difference so great as in the social relations. Jesus said, 'The children of this world marry and are given in marriage; but they which shall be accounted worthy to obtain that world, and the resurrection from the dead, neither marry nor are given in marriage.'

"We believe that we are doing God's will and that this is the beginning of heaven on earth; therefore we have abandoned marriage. It is certain that our lives have been happier and more peaceful since we did so. Marriage is a form of legality, and so far as women are concerned, it is a mild form of slavery. The husband feels that he owns his wife and can do with her as he wills. He looks upon this as his right, and if anyone dares interfere he is ready to shoot or stab. The history of marriage is filled with a succession of

such horrible jealousies.   Not a day
passes without its fresh instances.
With us there has been no such thing.
We have lived peacefully together.   It
is certain, therefore, that we have progressed in throwing off marriage.   But
if we escape from living under the law
we must be sure that we are living
under grace, and that our lives are
guided and controlled by inspiration.
We did not throw off legal restraints
until we knew certainly that the grace
of God was holding us in the right
path.

   " The love for woman is an encroach-
ing thing which, if given free rein,
would lead on to selfish, exclusive
claims, like those of marriage, whether
the marriage ceremony was had or not.
My impression is that such special
attachments as this between George
and Julia, except as they are entirely
overmastered and kept in check by
attractions and influences from heaven,
are stimulants that enlarge the appetite
faster than they satisfy it.   The passions and desires of a man grow strong

in proportion to the nursing they
receive, and out of proportion to the
possibilities of satisfaction. Mere freedom to associate would lead to a desire
for exclusive possession; exclusive
possession would not be enough without constant possession; and this, in
turn, is never satisfied without propagation; so you will have to seek satisfaction in the usual slavery of matri-
mony, where you would be farther than
ever from finding it.

"To come then directly to the practical point in such a case as this of
George and Julia, I would ask George
this question: If you find yourself
unable to resist the attraction for Julia,
so that you drift constantly in the
direction of special, exclusive love for
her, with a desire to possess her wholly,
against her will, what is the best course
for you now, after you have tried the
temptation and found out your infirmity, to draw nearer to her? or to recede
from her? We read of a 'wondrous
wise man' who first scratched his eyes
out by jumping into a thickset hedge,

and then scratched them *in* again, by
jumping 'with all his might and main'
into the selfsame hedge ; but we have
never seen with our own eyes any such
contradictory operations, and we may
well believe that it is prudent for us to
keep away from temptations that prove
too strong.

"But am I arguing against the possi-
bility of making a good thing of love?
By no means. Note the exception
which I made. I said, 'my impression
is that such attachments, *except as they
are entirely overmastered and kept in
check by attractions and influences from
heaven*, are stimulants that enlarge the
appetite faster than they satisfy it. I
admit, then, that the love for woman,
though it be like wine or brandy, an
enroaching stimulant, may be mastered
and made useful by the higher powers
of religious love. I do indeed believe
that love between the sexes, subdued as
it may be into a branch of the love of
Christ, and pursued as a science, with a
more eager thirst for improvement
than for present pleasure, will be some-

time like music, an ever-larging field of wholesome and refining discipline. Whether or not you come within the benefits of this exception and these conditions must be determined by the answers which you can give to such questions as the following :

" Has the love of Christ gained or is it gaining the supremacy over the love of woman in your heart? Are you now inclining as much towards spiritual life as you were a year ago? Or, to bring the question down to a lower sphere, are you pursuing love as a science and a means of improvement, or for its pleasures? Does it help you to improve in other things, or is it a means of dissipation ?

" I should like to hear from George himself, whether these views do not commend themselves to his sober judgment ? Do you not believe you would be happier to hold yourself in the attitude I have described ? "

George Stanley : " I am sure of .it I can now see clearly where I got off the right track, and as I feel that you are all kind friends who have come here from a desire to help me, I am willing to tell you all about it.

"I have loved Julia for a long time, and have been very happy in associating with her. Undoubtedly I might have continued so had I not become jealous of Mr. Scott. I saw that he felt attracted to Julia, and I began to fear she would love him more that she did me. I feel humiliated to have to make such a confession of littleness of heart. Since I fell under this temptation I have not known a happy moment, while before that my heart was light and free."

Father Temple: "Undoubtedly that is the truth about it. You did not stop to reflect that in our system you had nothing to claim. If Julia has given you her love, it was a gift, precious, no doubt, but not one you could claim if she chose to withhold it. She is her own mistress, owned by no one. By undertaking to set up a claim to her affections you offended her and really repelled what you wished to secure.

Julia is a true-hearted girl.   She wishes to keep her attention on improvement, and she has learned by experience that the claims of special love destroy her peace of mind.   She loves George, but she loves others, and must be left free.

"It used to be the fashion with novel-writers to represent their heroes and heroines as capable of loving only one person, and only once in their lives.   If the affair miscarried from any cause their existence was blighted.   They could never love again.   While there may have been some individuals constructed on this plan, it has never been true of men and women in general.   It all depends on the size of the heart, or, more accurately, of the soul.   To be godlike every man should love every good woman, and *vice versa*, using the term to denote the unselfish, brotherly feeling we are now talking about. Where this spirit rules there is no room for jealousy and strife.   If we find a person giving way to .those feelings we may know at once that he is off the track."

Mr. Scott: " I feel a great admiration of Mr. Stanlay for his candor and sincerity in stating his own difficulty as he did, and I will beg your indulgence while I say a few words about myself. Since I have been with you I, too, have been getting in love with Miss Fordham. Father Temple has just said that it was a natural thing to do, which relieves my mind somewhat. I have not said anything about this, even to Miss Julia, and it seems a queer thing to do to announce it first to this committee, she being present; but if truthtelling and opening the heart are the order of the day, I want to do my part. I will offer myself for criticism with Mr. Stanley, here and now. I am involved in the same matter, and although I have done no intentional wrong, I may need advice and criticism."

Father Temple: " That is the true position to take. If everyone will stop and say they want to do what will please God, there will be no trouble. The attitude now taken by these two men shows clearly the difference between our system and that of the world. If they were seeking Julia to marry her they would hate each other intensely. Here they can both love her while they feel a warm esteem for each other.

"I think it will be found that the most happiness will be derived from love of the opposite sex when it is not sought too directly, but comes spontaneously as a reward for something else we have done. Nobleness of heart will attract the best love."

Mr. Percival: "I believe that is true."

Many others: "So do I;" "That has been my experience;" "And mine also," etc.

Mother Temple: "The attitude George now takes of submission to the truth shows that he has a deep and honorable purpose, and I feel sure this experience will result in broadening his character. He will see that special love contracts the soul and leads to narrow, selfish feelings. It distorts

everything and leads the two persons
concerned to feel that they and their
affair are of more importance than all
other human interests, which is not
true."

Emily Floyd: "That is exactly the
point. The young women are learning
that they are happier not to give way
to the temptation to settle down into
exclusive relations with anyone. It is
sure to lead to trouble and worry of
mind.

Lily Millington: "I think some of
the older men are very pleasant companions because they do not set up
such exclusive claims, but leave their
friends perfectly free."

Father Temple: "The key to our
social system is *self-control.* That is
the foundation of our theory and
practice of "male continence." At
every stage of our experience self-
control must be maintained. There
must be no excesses or runaways.
Inspiration and sober judgment must
be able to say to the passions at any
time: "*Go no farther,*" with a certainty

of being obeyed. If the passions refuse to obey, we may know surely that we are going too fast, and must recede until thorough self control is restored. It is precisely this feature of our system which will prevent spurious imitations. If people attempt to live as we do before the spirit has conquered the flesh so as to give them this self-control, their passions will inevitably betray them. The world may think ours is too exacting a standard of life, but we know that no one can enter the kingdom of heaven until the good spirit does obtain full control of all his passions and appetites, and it is better to set up that standard here and now, than to drift along in self-indulgence, with the delusive hope that it will all come right somehow.

"In this case of George Stanley the safest way for him will be to turn his attention away from Julia for a time. He has been causing her worry and anxiety of mind, which he will regret, if he truly loves her, and he should now eave her free. Special love of this

kind makes a man think there is only
one lovable woman in the world, which
is very far from the truth. Some of
the middle-aged women are the most
charming companions I have known.
It would do George good to find this
out for himself."

Aunt Harriet: "I think this has
been a very edifying and instructive
conversation. It has not been a criticism quite in our usual form, but it is
calculated to help everyone of us as
well as George."

The Committee rose and the criticism was over. What a strange doctrine it had revealed! And yet, when
we reflect upon it, is it not stranger
still that the world should so jealously
maintain a system in which it is looked
upon as almost justifiable for one man
to kill another because they both happen to love the same woman? Nay,
worse still, a system in which the man
sometimes kills the woman he professes
to love, merely because she prefers
another! Has a woman not a right to

her own person, and to the control of her own destiny? How many are there in the world who know what true, unselfish, heavenly love is?

CHAPTER XII.

As the season advanced there was a great pressure of business at the Fruit House, which was located within easy walking distance from the dwelling. Vast quantities of ripe corn, tomatoes, peaches, and other crops were brought in daily to be canned; and notwithstanding a large force of hired workers was employed, the manager of that department found it necessary to call for special help from the members. "Bees" were organized nearly every evening, to keep the fruits from spoiling. The response to such calls was quite general. The members walked over to the factory immediately after supper, and worked for two or three hours as volunteers. These were sociable occasions. The men and women formed themselves into little groups around the work-tables. Seated on

benches or plain wooden chairs, with
agate dishes in their laps, some pared
the peaches and peeled the tomatoes,
while others packed them in the cans,
ready for the final cooking and sealing.
The hum of conversation and occasional laughter filled the room. An
enormous amount of work was accomplished in this way without fatigue.
Mr. Scott invariably attended these
"bees," and enjoyed them, for he made
many new and pleasant acquaintances
in this way. There was not much formality in the social intercourse of the
members. When any two met, a
simple greeting sufficed to start conversation.

An accident happened one evening
which threatened serious consequences.
A large and enthusiastic "peach bee"
had lasted until nearly ten o'clock,
when, all being finished for the day, the
members rose to return to the dwelling
together. The walk ran beside the
main highway for a short distance
before entering the grounds. As the
people sauntered leisurely along, still

engaged in conversations, suddenly loud cries were heard, as of persons in distress. Then a light carriage, drawn by two horses, came dashing down the road. The moon was shining brightly, and it could be plainly seen that it was a runaway. A man and a woman were seated in the carriage. The man was tugging at the reins, his feet braced against the dashboard, and shouting "Whoa! whoa!" at the top of his lungs. The woman clasped the man as tightly as possible, screaming hysterically. The horses were badly frightened, and were running fast. Mr. Scott sprang forward to try and stop them. He knew it would not do to get directly in front of the team, as he would inevitably be run over. Instead of this, he started to run in the direction in which the horses were going, keeping an eye over his shoulder, so that as they came up with him he was able to grasp the rein of the nearest one without being thrown off his feet. His weight served to check the animal, but the other horse continuing his frantic leaps, they were swerved suddenly out of the road, the carriage was overturned, and the occupants thrown out. This frightened the horses still more. They began to rear and kick, to free themselves, and would have succeeded had not a stalwart form at that instant seized the other horse. It was Henry Franklin, from whose iron grasp nothing could escape. Sooner than we can tell it, other hands joined these two; the horses were unhitched and quieted, and the carriage was righted. Fortunately the man and woman who had been thrown out, although badly bruised, were not seriously injured; and finding that neither the harness nor carriage was broken, they insisted on continuing their ride. Then Mr. Scott was discovered sitting in the grass by the roadside, groaning with pain. It was evident that he had been injured while stopping the runaways. The members gathered about him, and asked if he were badly hurt.

"One of the horses stepped on my foot, and I have wrenched my knee

so that it pains me very much," he
replied.

Henry Franklin and Arthur Dudley
lifted him carefully to a standing position.

"He cannot walk; we must carry
him," said Henry.

"Wait a minute," he added, as he
clasped hands with Arthur, so as to
make a very safe and comfortable chair.
"Now sit down, and put your arms
around our necks. That's right; here
we go," and they carried him as if he
were a child.

As he was raised aloft by the two
young stalwarts, Mr. Scott caught sight
of Julia Fordham, standing at a little
distance. Her eyes were fastened upon
him, full of the most tender solicitude,
and he thought he saw a tear glisten on
her cheek in the moonlight. Evidently
she felt for him a deeper regard than
she had heretofore permitted herself to
express by word or act. The thought
made his heart beat fast. This man,
who was having his first love experience under such unusual conditions,

who had been striving to suppress his own feelings, in order that he might not, by too great precipitation, lose what he so longed for, now found himself trembling with the force of his emotion. He saw Julia once again, as they carried him along the path through the little park. Her hat was thrown back on her shoulders, and she was still regarding him anxiously. How loving and gentle she looked, she who was usually so spirited and shy! The injured man forgot his hurt as he thought of her and vaguely hoped and wondered.

Happily Mr. Scott had sustained no more serious injuries than bruises and sprains, and in a few days he was quite comfortable. As he sat by his window one afternoon, he saw a group in the "Quadrangle" paring peaches for supper, and he called to them that if they would send him up a panful of the fruit and a knife, he would be glad to help.

"Here, Julia," said Mrs. Gregory, who had charge of the "bee," "won't you pick out some nice peaches, and carry them up to Mr. Scott? I dare say it will cheer him up to have something to do. The time goes slowly when one is confined."

Julia jumped up, and, after filling the pan, ran off with it. As she appeared to Mr. Scott, clad in a fresh muslin dress, blushing and smiling, and holding out the peaches, he thought he had never seen anything half so pretty.

"How do you do?" she said.

"I'm getting along nicely," he replied, as she wheeled a light stand up in front of him and placed the pan upon it. "At this rate I shall soon be about as usual. But why did you not bring two knives? Are you not going to sit by me, and talk to me?"

"I'll run back and get my knife and an apron for you. These ripe peaches will stain your clothes;" and away she tripped, bright as a fairy.

"My God!" exclaimed Mr. Scott to himself as he was again alone, "what a situation is mine! Here I am, only a probationary member of the Society, madly in love with this girl, who is a full member. I do love her as I never expected to love any woman. And I believe she loves me. Oh! the ecstacy of that thought! And yet I must exercise self-control. Self-control! How easy to resolve, how hard to perform! No doubt it will be best for me to have another talk with Father Temple soon. But I am going to tell that sweet girl how much I love her, though the heavens fall."

. . . . . .

Mr. Scott fully recovered his health just in time to take part in the first corn-cutting "bee" of the season. There were several large fields ready to be cut, and it was desirable to do the work quickly, as a frost would injure the stalks for fodder. It was therefore decided to make it a grand old-fashioned bee. The women were to be invited to assist. A general and rousing notice was given at dinner time, and as that meal was finished the stirring sound of a fife and drum was heard calling the people to assemble under

the large elm tree in front of the dwelling. Here each man armed himself
with a cutting-knife from a stack of
them which the head farmer had produced, ground sharp for the occasion.
Then all, men and women, formed
themselves in martial array, and, marching to the designated field, attacked
the corn like an army with banners
assaulting a fortress.

Imagine a hundred sturdy men, each
armed with a sharp and trusty blade,
hewing down the stalks, handing them
carefully to the hundred women, who
in turn placed them in stocks, where
certain skilled men rapidly bound them
in position, while a hundred lively
boys and girls gleaned the ears which
had fallen, tumbling about among the
ripe, golden pumpkins with which the
ground was thickly strewn, a band of
sutlers meantime carrying pails of cold
and refreshing drink among the workers.
Picture to yourselves the dash and
courage, backed by tremendous physical strength and endurance, with which
Henry Franklin, George Stanley,

Arthur Dudley, and the other young men led their several columns in the fray. There was a generous rivalry as to who should be first across the field. Picture the women dressed in the short skirts and pantalettes, with no corsets unnaturally compressing their waists, active, strong, and willing.

How the corn melted away? The effect was magical. One would imagine that the wind was laying it low, so rapidly it fell across the broad field. Could anyone call a two or three hours' effort of this kind, and in such company, *labor?* It was *sport*, keenly enjoyed. The beaming looks, the kindly smile on every face, the merry laughter, told of the ever-present love and good fellowship.

And when the work was done and all had marched back like a triumphant army to the dwelling, the men, in return for sisterly aid out of doors, helped the women to get supper, clear off the tables, wash and rinse the dishes, set the sponge for a huge

baking of bread, prepare potatoes
and other vegetables for cooking on
the morrow. One could then readily
see that this life had its compensa-
tions. The women were not made
household drudges, so they really
enjoyed helping the men in the fields
for an hour or two at a time when
the weather was fine.

When Mr. Scott heard this corn-
cutting "bee" announced he resolved
to make a practical attempt at self-
denial. He felt a strong desire to
secure Julia as a partner, and he thought
how pleasant it would be to work with
her. But he resolutely put this desire
aside and invited Aunt Millicent to be
his partner for the occasion. Aunt
Millicent was a woman of forty-five
years, and while she was not very strong
she had the gentlest, kindliest disposition imaginable. Mr. Scott resolved to
devote himself to making the day
pleasant to her. He took pains to
draw her out, and found she was possessed of much information. He carefully adapted his speed to hers, and

helped her in every way with so much grace and tact that she formed a very high opinion of him.

Now, these people's lives were bound so closely together that very many in the society recognized the effort Mr. Scott had made to act on principle, to make another happy instead of looking out for himself, and none of them was more pleased than Julia Fordham. She loved Mr. Scott, and she wanted every-one to know what a good man he was. She was proud of his effort, and when he invited her to take a walk with him that evening she assented with the best conscience in the world, and was so affectionate that he was repaid a hundred times.

The completion of the corn harvest was the signal for a grand picnic. This was held in a shady grove of maples which grew on the bank of the river. It was a great affair, a whole afternoon being given up to it. There was plenty to eat and drink, plenty of games and of social enjoyment, plenty of thanks-giving for blessings and prosperity

showered upon them.   The long tables,
covered with snowy linen, fairly groaned
under their load of such biscuits as only
Aunt Matilda could make, with sweet
butter and delicious honey in the comb.
At a convenient distance one or two
smart fires of wood gave opportunity to
roast ears of sweet corn which had been
planted late for this occasion and to
bake potatoes in the hot ashes.   These
fires were continually surrounded by
boys and girls, who held out the corn
on sharp-pointed sticks to roast it over
the embers.   Some of the older boys
and girls might also have been seen
taking a hand.   Who does not remember that corn cooked in this way, half
covered with ashes, the whole eaten
hot, has a flavor never found except at
an outdoor feast?   Seated or lounging
easily in groups on the green grass or
on rough board seats by the tables,
chatting, laughing, rehearsing funny
experiences, while bright young boys
and girls passed various dishes around,
all now relaxed thoroughly, and gave
themselves up to the pleasant influences
of the occasion.

There were songs, recitations, speeches, games, stories, until the dew began to fall, and several large wagons were driven down to take back the tables, chairs, and huge hampers.

CHAPTER XIII.

A FALSE INSPIRATION.

One Sunday, soon after the picnic we have described, it was noticed that Father Temple confined himself the whole day to his room. He did not even appear at meals, but Miss Emily Floyd was seen to cary him some light refreshments. Peeple asked Emily in low tones if he were ill? She replied, "No, not ill, but very, very sober and thoughtful."

When evening came and all assembled in the Hall for the usual eight o'clock meeting, it was noticed that he wore a look of unusal sternness as he entered and took his seat.

After the customary routine of newspaper report and the reading of correspondence had been gone through, no one paying much attention to them, Father Temple spoke:

"I have a very unpleasant duty to

perform this evening, yet the spirit of truth and sincerity compels me to it. I have prayed about it and reflected upon it until my way seems clear.

"You all know what my attitude has been, from the first day we settled here, in regard to proselyting for new members. There was at first some jealousy and distrust of us among our neighbors, on account of our all living together in a great unitary family, after we had abandoned monogamic marriage. This distrust was perfectly natural, because people did not want their sons and daughters exposed to any dangerous influences. I did not blame them, but I knew that after they became better acquainted with us this feeling would disappear, and I was able to fully reassure them by announcing through our paper that we would not attempt to proselyte nor to persuade anyone to join us. This was an honorable pledge given to the public by which we were bound to keep within our own lines, so far as our neighbors were concerned. I have always believed that God would send to us such as he had chosen to help carry on the work we have undertaken. New members have come to us as fast as we could assimilate and train them. This policy of non-interference with our outside acquaintances has been reaffirmed here in our meetings often enough for everyone to have thoroughly understood it, and there can be no excuse for having violated the pledge we gave.

" But it seems that one of our number has done this, not in one instance only, but in several; not openly, but without our knowledge. And all the time he has been doing it, he has professed the utmost loyalty to our doctrines and to me personally. He has also publicly made the most lofty pretentions to spiritual acquirements. To give such loud-sounding testimony while he was carrying on his proselyting tactics with outsiders, in person and by letter, in ways that would, if persisted in, endanger the friendly feeling the public now has for us, is a very serious matter, and one that calls for prompt and thorough treatment.

"It is right that we should make this case a warning and an example, so that others may learn not to stumble. Christ said : 'For it must needs be that offences will came, but woe unto him by whom the offence cometh.'

"The brother who has betrayed our confidence. in this way is Philander Koote. By a curious providence, the evidence of his insincerity and unfaithfulness came to me without my having sought it or having suspected Mr. Koote in any way. I have talked with him privately, and he has admitted the facts to be as I have stated them. We cannot temporize with evil. In this case we must invoke the searching power of criticism, the Spirit of Truth."

While listening to this terrible indictment, the members had fairly held their breath, so profound was the interest felt. The silence had been oppressive. But no sooner had Philander's name been mentioned as the culprit than every eye turned in search of him.   He did not occupy his accustomed seat in the front row of chairs, but had chosen an obscure corner, knowing this exposure was coming.   Murmurs of indignation could be heard on every side.   The unerring instinct of the people had long since detected the hollowness of Mr. Koote's religious pretensions, and this fact, added to his notorious laziness, now worked much to his disadvantage.

Father Temple continued: "I think we cannot spend this evening more profitably than by giving Mr. Koote a searching and faithful criticism here in the presence of the whole family.   Let us have a time of sincere truth-telling, such as will make the spirit of insincerity which he has harbored hide its head and leave us.   I invite everyone to speak freely what is given him or her to say.   The women are as much interested as the men.   We need not confine ourselves to this particular transgression, but should point out any other faults we have noticed.   But

before we begin I wish Mr. Koote
would step out here and take his accustomed seat near the center of the Hall.
He has kept himself well in front all
this time while he has been living in
hypocrisy, and it looks very cowardly
for him to get back there out of sight
just at this time. It is not Mr. Koote
that we are aiming at, but the evil spirit
which he has been harboring in secret.
We must make thorough work of it this
time. After we are sure that the evil
influence has been driven away from
among us, we can give our attention to
healing and comforting Mr. Koote, but
the surgery comes first."

In the awful pause which followed
these remarks the wretched Philander
arose, and picking his way between the
seats, advanced to his old place, where
every eye could find him, looking more
chapfallen and humiliated than ever
before in his life. Then the criticism
commenced in earnest.

EphraimDudley: "It is a matter of
great surprise and mortification to me
that one who has had the benefits of

this school for many years, one whom
Father Temple has trusted to write for
our paper, and to whom we have all
extended brotherly fellowship, should
have been deceiving us in this way.   I
cannot account for it.   It seems too.
gross a case of intentional wrongdoing
to believe one of our number guilty of.
He must have known that sooner or
later it would all come to the light.
How, then, could he have allowed himself to go on in such a course?   Mr.
Koote has been a stumbling-block to
our young people for a long time, and
must now have a radical change of
heart before he will be fit to mingle
with them."

Father Temple: "In regard to industry he has been a great stumbling-
block.   He has had a desire to write
for our publications, and I at first
thought he was going to be a help
to me in working out ideas which I
gave him; but I have noticed for
some time past that he has lost his
receptivity to me, and the consequence
is that his writings have been made

up of a lot of high-sounding but heavy sentences about the Jews and so forth, with no life or power in them. I don't want any more such help. Mr. Koote has been yielding to this temptation for a long time; and it may take as long to effect a cure as the disease has been running. He has been in a constant state of relapse and backsliding, and his moral nature is weak. It must be strengthened and built up by degrees.

"But though his moral nature is weak his body is strong, and there is no reason why he should not work. Laziness may be said to be at the root of his troubles. He hates to exert himself. If he had exerted himself to overcome temptation he would not have exposed us to this danger. The reform must commence by getting some energy into him."

Mr. Kinglake: "I have never taken any comfort in reading Mr. Koote's articles in the paper, but have supposed others did, so I said nothing against them. It seems there has been a good deal of pretension about him, in that as well as in spiritual things. This exposure leaves him pretty bare. When the swell and conceit are taken out there will not be much left. This is humiliating, no doubt, but it need not be wholly discouraging. None of us amount to very much without God in us. He is the source of all good. Mr. Koote's experience makes me doubly thankful that the rest of our members have been true to what we promised."

The criticism had opened with so much severity, and Mr. Koote was so well able to calculate what would follow, that he suddenly bethought himself of a bold course which might save some part of his reputation. Throwing off his attitude of dejection, he broke the rule of silence when under criticism, and spoke thus :

"I wish to say a few words in extenuation of what seems a great fault, but which, when rightly understood, may be found to have a justification. *I have felt inspired to do what I did.* If I have peculiar gifts and unusual powers of pleasing, these ought to be used for our cause. It can be shown that I have had great influence in interesting several persons in our doctrines. The ability to do that is a gift, and the desire to do it has, with me, been due to an inspiration. I have been told that there is a peculiar magnetism in my eyes. Ought we not to be free, each of us, to follow our inspiration, and use the faculties we have for the good of the cause?"

Father Temple: "Now we get at the root of the matter. I am glad the truth has come out. Here we have a member acting in defiance of our rules, breaking the pledge we gave the public, and claiming justification on the ground of inspiration. What is inspiration? We mean by it an influence from some unseen intelligence, and in claiming to be led by inspiration myself, I mean that I have found a way of getting at the mind of God so that I can know what course He desires me to take. But there are true and false inspira-

tions.   Inspirations from the true
source will not clash but will be har-
monious ; and they will be found acting
on the side of truthfulness and sincerity,
not in such a way as Mr. Koote has
been engaged in.   What he has just
said makes his case look worse than it
did before,   It is evident that he has
been led astray by a false inspiration,
and that a very serious work will have
to be done in him.   He must be cured
of his conceit and insincerity.

"Since this matter was brought to
my notice I have been considering
whether the society is not now large
enough.   It seems to me that it is, and
that we should now close the doors.
Instead of trying to proselyte for new
members, it will be better to limit our
numbers and try to make our society
as perfect as possible.   There are some
matters of the very highest importance
which we have not yet considered at
all.

"But let the criticism proceed.   The
women should say what they think of
Mr. Koote's claim to special magnetic

gifts. They will be the best judges of them. I don't want him influencing anyone to join us."

Mother Temple: "I have thought for a long time that there was insincerity in Mr. Koote. He has made swelling professions which his experience did not seem to justify. It is easy to recognize the good spirit in anyone. It is not characterized by egotism and swell, but by humility and softness of heart. Mr. Koote has been full of conceit and pride of intellect, with very little to base it on. This humiliation will prove a blessing to him if it produces softness of heart and sincerity.

Aunt Matilda: "Mr. Koote will have to change very much before we can have confidence in him again."

Lily Millington: "This exposure and criticism of Mr. Koote greatly strengthens my faith in the Providence over us. I did not know he had been doing wrong, but his spirit was repulsive to me. I could not bear to have him around."

Emily Floyd: "He has had a very

disagreeable way of trying to flirt with
the girls whenever he meets them.   It
is his habit to open his eyes as wide as
possible on every such occasion, I suppose in order to exercise the magnetic
charm he speaks of.   I hope he will not
do so any more.   If he knew how disagreeable he makes himself he would
not.   Women admire manhood and
courage, and no one cares to be hypnot-
ized or magnetized."

Mrs. Stanley: "I like what Lily
and Emily have said, and sympathize
very heartily with the whole criticism.
I will mention one other habit of his.
When Father Temple gives a discourse
in which he brings out some new theory,
Mr. Koote is apt to take it up and talk
about it in his superficial way, until
everybody is very much annoyed.   For
example, when Father Temple suggested that the spiritual center of man
is somewhere near the heart, instead of
in the brain, Mr. Koote seized upon
some of the terms used, and began
talking about his ' solar plexus ' and
his ' semilunar ganglion,' in a familiar,

off-hand way, as if he had known all about them since he was a child. He kept this up, week after week, until I positively dreaded to hear him allude to it."

Mr. Gregory: " Insincerity, or professing one thing and doing another, seems to have become a habit with Mr. Koote. It will be remembered that some time ago he announced a lecture in regard to eating and drinking. He began by referring to the antipathy the Jews had to eating pork, based on the Mosaic law, then spread out into a general condemnation of all meat-eating as being carnal and unbecoming in spiritually-minded men and women. He would even have excluded butter and cheese from the table, saying we could get all the oils and fatty material our systems require from nuts and other natural sources.

"Now, I like to have everyone free to think and say what he pleases, and Mr. Koote has a perfect right to hold and preach these ideas. But mark what happened! Not long after his

lecture we had a good meal of beefsteak with baked new potatoes and
all the trimmings. Although I believe
in vegetarianism in a general way, I
felt a great appetite for that beefsteak
when I came in from work and smelled
it cooking; and I entered the dining
room anticipating quite a treat, because
we have steak so seldom and I am very
fond of it. But I happened to seat
myself beside Mr. Koote, and I state
it soberly, as a fact, that I was unable to get a mouthful of steak until
the platter at our table had been
replenished several times. Mr. Koote
took care of it as fast as the waiter
could bring it on. I would not have
mentioned this if Mr. Koote had not
taken such extreme ground in his lecture. If he had said outright that he
was so desperately fond of beefsteak
that he could not possibly restrain
himself until he had eaten three or four
large pieces, I could have respected his
sincerity, whatever I might have
thought of his manners. I believe he
would have eaten half a roast pig that

day, even if Moses himself had been sitting opposite."

Father Temple : "We do not want to be that sort of reformers, preaching one thing and practising the opposite." ,

Henry Franklin : "My desire for Mr. Koote's salvation leads me to hope that he will now volunteer to milk. That would do more to convince me that he was really improving than anything I can think of. 'Faith without works is dead,' and the work which will do him the most good is to get up in the morning and milk."

Thus one after another laid bare poor Philander's failings and foibles, with a clearness and certainty that left no defence, and with a neatness won by much practice. There was no circumlocution, no waste of words. Everyone who aimed at him scored a point.

This profitable exercise lasted a full hour. It was easy to see that Mr. Koote was under deep conviction. Pale, with chin resting on his breast, there was no resistance left in him; and when the meeting broke up he retired to his

room, sore and downcast. Something
seemed to whisper in his ear:

"The way of the transgressor is
hard."

Mr. Koote had a good enough heart,
and was sincerely attached to Father
Temple at this time, but his nature was
shallow and conceited. His humility
did not last long. Subsequent events
showed that the desire to proselyte
remained in him, urging him to make
himself conspicuous.

This criticism was a revelation to Mr.
Scott. He saw that while the society
had few set rules or laws, claiming to be
guided rather by inspiration, yet the
lash of public opinion as used in these
criticisms, was a means of government
not to be trifled with. The conduct of
individuals had to conform to the will
of the Church. This discipline of Mr.
Koote was unquestionably severe, but
the transgression which drew it forth
was most flagrant. It was the only
such instance that Mr. Scott witnessed
in the society.

CHAPTER XIV.

It was rare that a death occurred in the Society of the Perfect Life from any other cause than old age. All the conditions surrounding the members were such as tend to promote longevity. Pure water from a living spring on the distant hillside was brought to the dwelling in underground pipes and distributed to every part. The ventilation of the buildings was carefully planned, and as they were warmed by steam the temperature was kept equable. The drainage was perfect. With good food, abundance of healthy exercise, entire freedom from care and worry, and an approving conscience, there was nothing to prevent these people from living out their allotted span but accidents and inherited tendencies to disease.

One of their number, Mr. Albert

Percival, had unfortunately injured himself by overlifting before he joined the society, since which he had never been entirely well and strong, although he was able to do light work. When the human system once becomes weakened from any cause all the evil influences which are abroad rush in to make it their prey. It was so in Mr. Percival's case. One thing after another happened to him to prevent his getting strong, until at length he contracted a severe cold which resulted in pneumonia. When he realized that his condition was critical and that he was like to die, he summoned his two children and their mother to his bedside, and with broken utterance addressed them thus :

" I may not recover from this attack. I fear that I am nearing my end, and if I should die I wish you to observe these things : We must all be reconciled to God's will in regard to us. If He takes me away from you, trust Him still, and do not give way to sadness or sorrow. Do not wear mourning garments, but wear flowers instead. Let my funeral be as simple as possible, with very few of the customary formalities. We shall be separated for only a few short years, when you will all join me again. I shall watch over you if so I am permitted. My strength is going. I cannot see clearly. Now let me take each of your hands in mine and so bid you good bye. You will be among loving friends who will watch over you and care for you. I shall feel that you are safe. God-bye, and may God bless you."

There was a slight pressure of the hand, then he closed his eyes and spoke no more.

It was arranged as he had requested. The funeral was very simple, no outside clergyman being summoned. The members gathered in the Hall, where the body lay, to take a last look at the features of their departed brother. While Mrs. Percival and her children could not refrain from weeping, they struggled bravely with their grief, in an effort to do as he had bidden. The other members seemed deeply affected. It was evident that they had loved Mr.

Percival, and felt the loss of his companionship. They joined in singing several hymns, Father Temple made a few remarks, then a procession was formed, and the body was laid away in its last resting-place in the little cemetery of the Society.

A few hours later the death was made the subject of conversation in the evening meeting. Mr. Edward Percival, after expressing his thanks to the Society for the kindness shown by everyone during his brother's illness, said:

"It is a great comfort to me at this time that brother Albert could die without feeling any anxiety for his family. He was wholly at rest about them, and died in peace. If he had not joined our Society he would have suffered, as so many others do, from anxiety lest those who were naturally dependent on him, having no longer anyone to protect and support them, might be imposed upon by selfish persons, and perhaps come to want. He also felt entire peace and rest as to himself, because he had been striving, to the best of his ability, to please God, and he believed that God loved him, and would receive his spirit."

Father Temple : "Death is the last enemy to be overcome. We can look forward to a time when the immortal part of man shall have triumphed over mortality, so that death will no longer have power over us. Exactly how it will come about is a great mystery, which we cannot fully understand; but as we progress in a knowledge of spiritual philosophy, it will become plain to us. We can form some conception of how the body may be changed so as to be no longer subject to what we call 'natural laws,' by considering Christ's resurrection body. When He rose on the third day His body was changed. It still partook of the mortal nature, in that it appeared much as before. The Lord walked and talked with His disciples, and even ate with them by the seashore, as told by St. John. Yet He was able, with this same body, to appear before them in an inner room, the doors

being closed, which shows the spiritual
nature of His body. I look upon spirit
as a very refined form of matter, able
at will to traverse the grosser forms
amid which we live. This conception
will help us to form true ideas of what
our heavenly state will be. We are
created in the image of God, and
our spiritual, immortal bodies are the
counterparts of our mortal bodies. I
believe that when two of us meet in the
next world we shall at once recognize
each other, and appear so natural that
we shall hardly realize that we are
spirits. Some people think of the spirit
as merely a bit of shapeless vapor, a
cloud, an essence, or an intangible and
unsatisfactory something. I once heard
a clergyman preach a sermon in which
he compared our spirits to vapor floating in the skies. I believe our spiritual
bodies will be imbued with form, substance, and all the intelligence and
feeling we now possess. It is merely
the mortal husk which is laid aside at
death. When the soul is at peace with
God, this change should cause no fear
or pain."

Mr. Stanley: "Those are very interesting thoughts in regard to the nature of our spiritual bodies. We must accustom ourselves to think of them as not differing from our mortal bodies except as spirit differs from external matter. The various forms of matter with which we are familiar vary greatly as to their density, gravity, and other qualities. Water will enter the pores of wood, and, being fluid, can also percolate through the rocks. Atmospheric air is a yet more delicate form of matter, able to penetrate many seemingly solid substances. Beyond air we have electricity, a still more subtle form. It was considered very mysterious and dangerous for a long time, but electricians now manufacture it, handle it, and direct it where they will, just as other mechanics handle water. It is a fluid which will run up hill as readily as down, and can penetrate almost anything. Our spirits are probably only a still finer form of matter. God is a spirit, yet He is all-powerful. It will do us good to reflect on these things,

and form true conceptions.   It will rob
death of its terrors."

Mother Temple: "I feel a deep love
and sympathy for Mrs. Percival and
her children.   We can all surround
her with our fellowship so that she
will not suffer from a sense of bereave-
ment.   I was thinking this afternoon
what a great insurance we are to each
other.   All our property is pledged
to the equal support of every member,
the little ones as well as the old ; and
not only that, but we have here a hundred strong and able men ready to protect and care for those who need it."

Mr. Pendell: "Our system is really
the best form of insurance yet discovered.   In ordinary life-insurance, when
the insured dies, the amount is paid to
the beneficiary in money, but there is
nothing to prevent unscrupulous persons from getting it away by trickery
or fraud, or to prevent its being lost by
foolish investments.   The personal
support and protection of many living
friends is worth more than any sum of
money.

Mrs. Percival: "I feel very thankful for God's goodness to me and my children. When we joined the Society I did not expect that Mr. Percival could live more than a few months. The doctors had prepared me for his death at any time, yet in this home his life has been spared many years. I also feel a deep sense of gratitude to every one of you for your kindness and sympathy. I am not left alone, nor are my children fatherless."

Father Temple: "Every man of us will be a father to those children. They shall not want for care or love."

Mr. Gregory: "They shall not; and every one of us will be a brother to Mrs. Percival."

Aunt Harriet: "Holding the views we do about death, we need not put on mourning raiment and go about with sad countenances when one of our number is taken away. If God's will is done we ought not to feel sad about it, but to rejoice that we can believe on Him."

Mr. Stanley: "The fashion of

mourning is kept up in deference to a foolish public opinion. When a wife loses her husband, unless she put on black raiment and weep overmuch the gossips will say 'Oh, she did not love him after all.' How foolish! As if putting on or off certain robes could show how much we have loved those who died."

Father Temple: "It is not only foolish to think so much of what the neighbors will say, but the fashion of having very solemn, impressive funerals, in which the minister seeks to intensify the grief of the mourners by his remarks, followed by this fashion of mourning, tends to make even more severe the inevitable nervous shock caused by the death. These fashions are therefore prejudical to the health of the living, while they do no good to anyone."

This was not mere formal talk on the part of the members. As the days wore on they did as they had said. A thousand little things were planned to comfort Mrs. Percival and her children, and to break the force of the blow which had fallen. As the weeks rolled into months and the months into years, the same watchful and tender care was maintained. In this system it seemed as if the heart of each member touched every other heart, so closely were they bound together.

CHAPTER XV.

THE CHILDREN.

It happened that about the middle of November Miss Julia Fordham was assigned to a position in the "Children's House." It must be known that in the Society of the Perfect Life all the children under twelve or fourteen years of age lived apart from the adult members, in a comfortable house of their own which adjoined the main dwelling; but they took their meals in the common dining-room. Their building was so arranged, with a large and well-shaded playground in the rear, that their noise would not disturb the older people.

When a family with children joined the Society, the youngsters were at once put to live in the Children's House, where they were soon extremely well contented with their fifty or sixty little playmates. A group of five or six caretakers attended to the wants of them all, thus relieving the parents entirely. This arrangement went far to destroy the spirit of family selfishness which might otherwise have led parents to be always on the look-out for their own children. They were all regarded as the children of the Society, to be equally loved and protected. Those who had no children of their own felt as rich as those who had many. They could take their turn in living with them, and very often warm attachments sprang up where there was no blood relation.

The responsible heads of this group of caretakers were called respectively the "Father" and "Mother" of the "Children's House." One of the young women usually served on this staff a few weeks at a time, her duties being to entertain and care for the smallest children during a part of each day. She could take them to walk, read to them, tell them stories, or teach them little games; and must see that they were always clad suit-

ably to the weather. This was the
position to which Julia was now
assigned.

One pleasant afternoon when the
sun shone with genial warmth as if
to defy the coming cold, she had taken
her little charges to the extreme end
of the lawn, where stood a group of
tall pine trees, and in their shade two
rustic seats. The ground underneath
the trees was thickly strewn with dry
pine straw, making a natural carpet,
on which the children played. They
had several of the tiniest little wheelbarrows and carts, in which they were
gathering pine cones, to be afterwards
piled in what was to them a huge
mound. Minette had come out with
Julia, and the two now sat on one of
the rustic seats watching the little ones
and chatting meanwhile. It was a
peaceful, innocent scene, such as the
eye of a painter would love to catch.

Just then Mr. Scott was seen coming
down the walk with light and rapid
step, swinging his arms and expanding
his lungs with deep inhalations of the

bracing autumnal air. Suddenly he came upon the little group in the pines.

"Halloo!" he cried, "if this isn't a pretty sight! May I stop and view your Lilliputians at work, Julia?"

"Certainly, I have been enjoying it myself," she replied as she made room for him on the seat between her and Minette. "They are such gentle children, and they play so kindly together. They never quarrel. See what a mountain of pine cones they are making. Aren't they industrious?"

"Yes, indeed. They are examples. I suppose you get to feel quite motherly, do you not, caring for so many little ones?"

"Yes, I find it a good, useful experience."

"The children of the Society all seem to be very healthy. Have there been any deaths among them?"

"I have lived here eight years," said Minette, "and there has been no death among the children during that time. Have you known of any, Julia?"

"No," replied Julia, "there has been

no death, nor even any severe sickness.
Their conditions are so good that nothing is ever the matter with them. They
are well clothed, eat nothing but the
most wholesome food, never sit up late,
and play out of doors a great deal."

"It is remarkable that there should
not have been a single death among so
many in eight years," said Mr. Scott.
"I believe that, according to the vital
statistics of ordinary society, there
would have been ten or twelve deaths,
if these children had been no better off
than the average. It is a strong point
in favor of your system."

"Why do you say 'your system'?
asked Julia. "Why not say 'our system'? Are you not one of us?"

"Not yet, in the full sense. I have
not signed the Covenant, but am here
only on probation for a year. I am
looking forward to the time when my
case will be decided."

"I do not see why you need wait a
full year, unless you choose to," said
Minette. "You have made many
friends here."

"It is pleasant to be told that, but some of my friends outside felt so unreconciled to my coming here that I thought, for the sake of harmony and good-feeling, it might be wiser for me to wait a year, and report to them my impressions of this place and the people, before taking the final step. I don't mind saying that it will cost me some self-denial to wait so long."

"Why do your friends think so ill of us?" asked Julia.

"They do not think ill of this Society in particular, but are so very conservative that they distrust all new ideas. I am going to give them a great shaking up when I go back to New York, at the end of the year. But let me ask you a little more about the children. I am much impressed by the fact that there has been no death among such a number in eight years. Have they not had the common infantile diseases, such as measles, whooping-cough, and scarlet fever?"

"There have been cases of those diseases here," replied Minette, "but the

children attacked were isolated and
carefully nursed, so that none proved
fatal. In fact, the little ones do not
seem to be easily overcome. They rally
quickly whenever they are attacked."

- "It is wonderful, wonderful," said Mr.
Scott, as if in deep meditation. "If
the world could only realize how easily
they might escape from many of the
miseries they now endure, it would seem
that they must, as rational beings, bestir
themselves, and put away their narrow-
minded prejudices. When I recall the
sight of the swarming little ragged,
unhealthy things in the crowded streets
of the large cities, and contrast their
appearance with the children playing
yonder, I wonder that the old system
can continue a day. But we must not
despair; changes will come in God's own
time."

"One nice thing about these children
is that they are so intelligent and obe-
dient," said Julia. "Children naturally
learn readily from each other; they have
their own public opinion, just as much
as grown folks do, and if that opinion

is in favor of obedience and respect, they all learn it, just as they might otherwise learn to be mischievous and unmanageable. We have a little meeting with them after breakfast every morning, and talk to them about beginning the day right. In that way they are easily controlled."

"Then you do not have to punish them?"

"Rarely ever. If one of them should become heedless or show ill-temper, he might be made to sit down by himself a little while and think it over. That would correct it. Before long a good, pleasant look would shine out of his little face, and he would then say he was sorry he had had a bad spirit, and go to play again with the others."

"Not a very severe form of discipline," said Mr. Scott, smiling. "I used to get soundly spanked for rather light offences when I was a little fellow.

"But come, Julia," he added, "will you not go to walk with me over by the spring? I have a plan I would like to unfold to you."

"I am afraid I cannot leave the children ; it is my duty to attend to them,"
she replied.

"I am at leisure, and will take charge
of them until supper time for you," said
Minette, "so you can go as well as
not."

"Oh, thank you," said Julia, and she
started off with buoyant step.

CHAPTER XVI.

A NOTABLE LECTURE.

As the season advanced and the out-door work was closed up in preparation for winter, all the members of the Society began to arrange for a time of vigorous study and improvement. Classes were formed in all the common branches, such as mathematics, astronomy, history, geography, chemistry, and languages. Several of the elderly people began the study of Greek, that they might be able to read the Testament in that original. Classes were also formed for the study of vocal and instrumental music, and for dancing. It was the custom to have several courses of lectures during the winter, and to present a play on the stage at least once a month.

The enthusiasm with which the members took hold of all these improving things made the winter seem to pass all too quickly. Each one chose what

he or she would study, and the classes
were arranged accordingly. Nothing
could have been more pleasing than to
see the old and young, the men and
women, mingling thus. It made the
elderly ones feel young again, and the
young often found occasion to feel
increased respect for the old. It was
found that a quiet old gentleman, who
was seldom noticed, could spell down
every one of the others in the public
contests. Another had an excellent
knowledge of astronomy, and so on.
The plays given by the members were a
source of endless mirth and enjoyment.

Father Temple announced that, on
the twentieth of February, he would
deliver a lecture which would, he hoped,
mark a new era in their development.
Much curiousity was felt as to what
this could be, and when the hour for
its delivery arrived every member was
in his seat. This lecture was so characteristic of the man and of his movement,
that the reader will demand it verbatim.
Here it is :

"SCIENTIFIC PROPAGATION."

"To prepare your minds for what I am about to present to you, let me recall briefly how we have been led by inspiration to establish this home. We did not foresee all the difficulties we would have to encounter, nor the exact outcome of our efforts. We began in a small way with such men and means as God gave us, and we have built up a little Society on true principles, which will stand for an example to the world. We have established industries of our own which are now so large and prosperous that our future income seems assured. That was the first step, to become self-supporting.

"We have also established schools of our own such as give us all the advantages of the most favored classes, and our young people show the good effects of · this culture. We were a good average lot of people, as good as the ordinary run of authors, clergymen, farmers, and mechanics, perhaps, and by our living together in this unitary household we have risen rapidly in the scale of broad intelligence and refinement.

"A far greater achievement than these have been to learn to live harmoniously together as we do. That required refinement of spirit and the weeding out of selfishness. A great work has been done in us, and we now live in closer and deeper spiritual fellowship than the world knows anything about.

"In all these things we have laid a broad and strong foundation for what is to come. The past has been only a time of preparation for the greater things to which we are now called. Our system, in order to be a true and enduring example, must be complete, providing for every human interest, both material and spiritual. It is not yet thus complete, but the most important step of all is the one I will now ask you to consider.

"*We have made no provision for the begetting and rearing of children for the Society.*

"I have given much thought to this subject for several years past, but not until recently has my mind become clear as to our true course in regard to it. We cannot follow the fashions of the world, having put aside marriage as being the stronghold of selfishness; nor do we wish to do so, for there is, I believe, a better way.

" It should be our purpose to produce the finest possible type of children, not for the selfish gratification of the parents, but for the good of the world. To understand how we may do this we must study, in a scientific, truth-loving spirit, the principles which underlie the propagation of improved types of any species. We must put aside all mawkish sentiment and all false modesty, and seek earnestly for the truth.

" Leading thinkers have in all ages recognized the analogy between skillful propagation of animals and of man. More than two thousand years ago Plato represented Socrates as urging on his pupils this analogy, and the duty resulting from it, in the following conversation :

" 'Tell me this, Glaucon ; in your

house I see both sporting dogs and a great number of well-bred birds ; have you ever attended to their pairing and bringing forth young ?'

" ' How ?' said he.

" ' First of all, among these, though all be well-bred, are not some of them far better than all the rest ?'

" ' They are.'

" ' Do you breed, then, from all alike ; or are you anxious to do so, as far as possible, from the best breeds ?'

" ' From the best.'

" ' But how ? from the youngest or the oldest, or from those quite in their prime ?'

" ' From those in their prime.'

" ' And if they are not thus bred, you consider that the breed, both of birds and dogs, greatly degenerates ?'

" ' I do,' replied he.

" ' And what think you as to horses,' said I, ' and other animals ; is the case otherwise with respect to them ?'

" ' It were absurd to think so,' said he.

" ' How strange, my dear fellow !'

said I. 'What extremely perfect goverment must we have if the same applies to the human race!'

" 'Nevertheless it is so,' replied he.

" Now the fact that this great truth was seen so long ago, while no steps have been taken to secure a scientific method of improving the human race by means of propagation, shows that there has been some great and insurmountable obstacle in the way. Every reasonable person will admit the supreme importance of the subject, and we cannot doubt that it would have been reduced to a practical science long before this if men had been free to act.

" *The great obstacle which has held the world back is marriage.*

" Flowers, fruits, and all kinds of domesticated animals have been wonderfully improved by skillfull breeders. It has been done by careful and scientific selection of individuals for mating. The cart horse and the race horse sprang from the same stock. They have been developed into widely different types by this means. So one type of cow has been bred for giving a large quantity of milk, and a very different type for beef.   Wonderful results have been achieved in the breeding of sheep, swine, pigeons, and, in fact, of all domestic creatures.   It seems to be possible to produce any given form or color, by selecting and mating the parents scientifically. A skillful breeder of pigeons used to say that he could produce any given feather in three years, but it would take him six years to obtain head and beak.   It is said of this man that he used to spend two or three days in examining, consulting, and disputing with a friend which were the best of five or six birds.   Another eminent breeder told a friend that he always deliberated for several days before he matched each pair.

"This shows us how science. deals with the subject.   Men take advantage of the law that like begets like, that all traits, both good and bad, are trans-missible, to greatly improve all the lower animals. But man himself, the most important being of all, having no visible superior to compel him to the scientific course in breeding his kind, has not made a similar improvement. The institution of marriage has not permitted a wise selection of individuals for mating. Mariages are brought about by sentiment. A young man and a young woman fall in love and marry, without giving a thought to what sort of children they are likely to have. It may be that their children are ill-formed, weak, and sickly; they keep on breeding, nevertheless.

" In the case of man this matter is of vastly greater importance than with the animals, because intellectual and spiritual traits are hereditary, as well as physical traits. Criminals should never be allowed to propagate. It is recorded that of the direct descendants of one woman who was a notorious criminal, the astonishing number of one hundred and eighteen persons were convicted of crime and imprisoned. That illustrates the influence breeding has on the elevation or lowering of human character. To be born right is the most important thing that can happen to a man.

"Those people who cling so tenaciously to old institutions, no matter how productive of evil they may be, or how much they obstruct the world's progress, may contend that it would be wrong to interfere with what is called 'natural selection' of human mates, even while the wonderful results of artificial, scientific selection in breeding animals and birds are freely admitted. It is fashionable to exalt the special magnetic attraction between a young man and a young woman into the highest place, as though it were the loftiest and most worthy sentiment they were capable of. But even this fashion is changing. The 'love in a cottage' idea is giving place to a prudent outlook in regard to money. It would be only a step farther to take a prudent outlook in regard to what sort of children any proposed union is likely to produce. As to the naturalness of this, I contend that many things which are natural for man are not natural for the brutes, such as wearing clothes, living in houses, and cooking our food.

Nobody would think for a moment that we ought to be governed in those things by the custom of animals, neither should we in such higher matters as propagation. We must use our brains, and try to produce the best results.

"I have said that marriage is the institution which has prevented the human race from enjoying the enormous benefits of scientific propagation. Consider, now, how wonderful it is that we have been led by inspiration to discard marriage. We had no thought of its influence on breeding, but we threw it off because it proved to be such a stronghold of selfishness. Now we, alone of all people on the earth, find ourselves free to apply true scientific principles to the breeding of our children. We have devoted our lives and our energies to establishing a true form of society, and I esteem it a wonderful providence which makes it possible for us to set the world an example in scientific propagation. It will make our system complete, and round out our career,

"The study of this subject ought to be a great incentive to individual improvement. Those who are ambitious to take part in propagation should exercise themselves mightily to get rid of their bad traits and to strengthen their good ones. We must strive to be healthy and vigorous physically, and to develop all the nobler qualities of our nature. The work of selection will probably be left to a judicious committee, and they will naturally begin by marking off all who are, from any cause, not fit. Such traits as laziness, conceit, and marked selfishness would disqualify a person just as surely as if he were scrofulous or consumptive.

"I look upon it as the noblest ambition we can set before ourselves to produce children perfect in mind, in disposition, and in body. As we advance in years so that our own activities begin to wane, what pride and happiness we can feel if we are able to see such a class growing up in the Society. The children we have are very good, but I believe wonderful results can be produced by applying scientific principles to the selection of parents for mating.

"I have presented these ideas in order that we may all study them together. We must all feel united and sure of our position before we take any practical steps. It will be the supreme test of our unselfishness, but I believe we are now sufficiently advanced to undertake it. We will make haste slowly, and ask God to give us wisdom and grace."

CHAPTER XVII.

MODERN NICODEMUSES.

The radical departure from old customs which Father Temple had made,
and the fearless, sincere way in which
he published the particulars of his faith
and practice through the medium of his
weekly paper, attracted to him many con-
fidences from persons outside his society
who would never have been suspected
of harboring a single idea which was not
exactly in line with the old ways and
usages. Letters were frequently received from bright, thinking people,
asking for more details of the new life,
expressing unbounded admiration of
what had already been accomplished
by the society, and very often making
confessions of personal experiences in
marriage and out of it, such as gave the
members views of ordinary society
quite suprising. Many were the tales
of married infelicity, of strange incom-

patibilities of disposition and temper, and of heartfelt longing to be free from the yoke, which were told to Father Temple and his people.

As the winter months rolled by and the genial month of May came again, a singular coincidence served to impress upon the mind of Mr. Scott the exeeding flimsiness of the apparent loyalty to old traditions which people hold up in front of them as a shield. It happened that a letter was received on the same day from each of three prominent men in New York City, asking permission to visit the society. One of these letters was from a distinguished clergyman, another from a well-known physician, the third from an editor of note. It would be obviously improper to give their names, as it was their evident desire to make quiet, unheralded visits. The clergyman wrote thus:

"Rev. Robert Temple.

"*My Dear Sir:*—I have for several years been somewhat familiar with your doctrines and can assure you that while I would not be permitted to preach them from my pulpit, yet I cannot but feel in my heart that you are right. Your beliefs in regard to the Origin of Evil, the Second Coming of Christ, and the necessity of our being really saved from sin, are so manifestly true that there is no gainsaying them. Yet the world is not ready to accept them, and, humiliating though it be, a hired clergyman can only preach what is acceptable to his flock.

"In regard to your social and domestic arrangements I am not fully informed, and I feel some curiosity to observe for myself the practical workings of your system. To this end I write to ask if I may be permitted to make you a brief visit with my wife. We are going to Niagara Falls soon, and could arrange to stop over with you for a day or two. I would like to time our journey so as to arrive at your place on the 20th inst., as I understand this will be before your regular season for receiving visitors opens, and we could therefore have a quiet opportunity to study you by ourselves.

Very sincerely yours,

———— ————."

The learned physician wrote as follows:

"REV. ROBERT TEMPLE,

"*My Dear Sir:*—I am at the present time engaged in writing a book in which I shall treat more especially of nervous diseases such as are caused and aggravated by hurry, worry, and the high pressure of our modern ways of life; and having read an account of your society, in which the conditions and environments are all so very different from those that obtain in the great world, I beg to ask if you can conveniently accord me the satisfaction of a short visit, in order that I may observe your people and their ways of life for myself? God knows the world has need of some new way of living, if we are to preserve any health at all. It would be most convenient for me to take a fast train which reaches your station about noon, leaving here early in the morning of the 20th inst. My wife wishes to accompany me, as she feels much interest in your people. Kindly advise me by return mail, and oblige."

The editor couched his request in these words:

"REV. ROBERT TEMPLE,

"*My Dear Sir:*—I would ask the privilege of making you a short visit with my wife, for the purpose of studying your system, of which I have read several accounts that interested me deeply. I do not ask this with any intention of writing about you myself, but because I feel a profound admiration of the

courage and skill with which you have con-
ducted the experiment thus far, and a hope
that it may lead the world up to better things.
If acceptable to you my wife and I would
leave here by a train which will reach you
late in the afternoon of the 20th inst.   May
we come ?

Yours truly,

——— —————.''

Strangely enough, Mr. Scott had
known each of these three men quite
well when living in New York, and had
met two of them abroad.   So when
their letters were read in evening meeting, and the odd fact·that they should
have all hit upon the same date for their
visits was alluded to, he foresaw an
amusing situation.   He knew very well
that, while the writers were quite sincere in their expressions, they would
scarcely wish to have it known how
much they sympathized with the new
movement, because of what their distinguished acquaintances might say.   But
he decided to keep his own counsel, for
the sake of observing how these people
would carry themselves when they

should unexpectedly meet at the Society. He knew that they were well acquainted with each other, so there would be no escape. Father Temple sent favorable replies to the writers, cordially inviting them to come on the day named.

The clergyman and his wife were the first to arrive on the twentieth, coming on an early train. Finding the coast clear, they started out on a tour of inspection, under the friendly guidance of "Aunt Julia." They visited the kitchen, laundry, and all the public rooms, and after spending an hour in the flower-gardens, engaged a team and drove to the silk factory.

Scarcely had they gone when the physician and his wife alighted from another train. The doctor was a bustling, energetic little man with rotund form and bald head. After eating luncheon, he was taken in charge by Mr. Pendell, and, with pencil and note-book in hand, was soon racing about from one place to another, asking questions at the rate of three or four a minute.

Three hours later the editor and his wife arrived. The day was then too far spent to allow of sight-seeing, so they retired to their room to rest and prepare for supper. So it happened that neither of the couples met until they entered the dining-room and were seated together at the visitors' table. Then there was a mutual recognition, somewhat embarrassed salutations, and notwithstanding these people were too well-bred to betray the surprise they really felt, there was a slight bowing of heads over teacups, as the comical aspect of the situation dawned upon them. Mr. Scott, who sat at a table in another part of the room, where he could observe them, had much ado not to laugh outright, but he managed to suppress the disposition, resolving to make himself known to them after supper.

When the meal was over, the visitors all retired to the reception-room, actuated by a common desire to make explanations. A little later Mr. Scott also entered the room. The clergyman and his wife were seated on a large, old-fashioned sofa, covered with hair-cloth. The doctor and his wife and the editor and his wife had drawn large rocking-chairs up in front of the sofa, so they were all assembled in a little group, and so occupied in what they were saying that they did not notice Mr. Scott when he first entered. As he approached them, the clergyman was saying:

"Yes, I had heard so much about this strange society, that finding I could spend a few hours here without losing my Western connections, I decided to run up and look it over. Of course I have no sympathy with such radical ideas, but nowadays a clergyman must know what the world is."

"Thas is so," chimed in the editor; "we cannot properly criticise any new development such as this until we understand what it is, and what its claims are."

"My visit is merely in the interest of science," said the physician. "I am here to study the conditions which relate to health, and to compare them with ordinary conditions. I do not concern myself with the religious doctrines or social theories of the society."

As the little man said this he happened to glance over his shoulders and saw Mr. Scott. Recognizing him instantly he leapt to his feet, grasped him by the hand, and in a loud, hearty voice exclaimed :

"Good evening, Mr. Scott, when did you arrive? Are all the rest of our New York friends on the way here, or what has happened to send you on alone?"

At this they all laughed heartily, and shook Mr. Scott by the hand.

"I might retort by asking how it happens that three such representative men from my native town should resolve to visit this quiet place together?" he replied. "Are you all turned Perfectionists, and have you come to join?"

"Lord bless you! no," replied the little doctor. "We did not come

together, but met here quite by chance.
The strangest part of it is that each of
our visits is in a manner accidental.
One lost a train, the others found themselves thrown this way by unusual
circumstances, and so here we are,
determined to make the best of it.
Strange, is it not? What accident,
drove you here?"

"What you tell me about yourselves
is, indeed, quite surprising." said Mr.
Scott. "I have been living here some
months myself, as a probationary member, and when I heard your letters read
in our evening meeting, asking permission to visit us, I judged that your
coming would be by calm design, and
not at all by accident. How do you
explain that?"

"Ho! ho! ho!" laughed the little
doctor, clapping his hands, "here's a
go, sure enough. We may as well own
up, all of us, and leave off this hypocrisy. Mr. Scott can see through us if
he has read our letters."

"That is true," said Mr. Scott. "It
seems to me that you worthy people are

suffering from such an abject fear of each other's opinions that you scarcely dare tell the truth. In your hearts you sympathize with the doctrines taught by Father Temple, and you would un-doubtedly enjoy living here. If you only had the courage to speak out your real views, you would find you have nothing to fear, as half the world is heartily tired of the old system, and ready for something better."

" I guess that is pretty nearly the truth," said the editor. "We are afraid of each other. But how does it happen that we find you in the position of a probationary member, friend Scott? You seem to be quite an advanced student of the new system."

" Yes, I have lived among these peo-ple for nearly a year, and the more I see of them, the better I like them. I hope you will all remain here long enough to understand them. Now that there is no further occasion for your keeping on your disguises, why not candidly and fearlessly investigate? I will do all I can to aid you."

"Thank you," said the editor. "I, for one, will accept your offer."

"So will I," said the physician.

"And I," said the clergyman.

"If Mr. Scott can afford to spend a year here, I do not think a day or two will harm us," said the clergyman's wife.

So it was settled that they would all remain. Finding that Mr. Scott was acquainted with these people, Father Temple requested him to give up his time to them, and to arrange whatever entertainments he thought proper for the evening hours. As master of ceremonies, he gave one entire evening to music. The orchestra played the overtures to "William Tell" and to 'Zampa," a set of waltzes by Lanner, and a work entitled "La Bambinella," by one Carolus Swift, a member of the Society. The children sang several pretty songs and performed their little pantomime. Miss Minette Pendell sang the "Angel's Serenade," by Braga, Hugo Fairfax playing the violin obligato with great delicacy ; and Miss Julia

Fordham rendered several piano solos most acceptably. Mr. Scott was really proud of these performers, who, being in the main self-taught, might easily have been taken for professionals. Performing together daily had given them a smooth and agreeable execution. The doctor was passionately fond of music, and grew positively enthusiastic. The lady visitors declared, with one voice, that the children were better trained than any they had ever seen before.

The next evening was given up to a dance in the Hall. The chairs and tables were stacked away in the ante-rooms, and the floor was carefully pre-pared. They danced good old-fashioned quadrilles, country dances, reels, etc., not having become versed in the mod-ern round dances. The doctor and his wife took part in this healthy exercise, and so did the editor and his wife ; but the clergyman could not permit such an indulgence, though he looked on in an interested way. It was a novelty to see the ladies of the society dance in their short dresses and pantalettes.

The third and last evening was spent in the ordinary way, the evening meeting occupying the hour from eight till nine o'clock. There was the customary news report and reading of correspondence, followed by religious conversation.

By this time the visitors had begun to feel the atmosphere of brotherly love and fellowship which reigned here. Every possible kindness had been shown them; they had been accorded every means of studying the system, and when, at length, the hour for their departure arrived and they were standing together on the platform of the railway station, the little doctor turned to the clergyman and the editor, and said, as he pointed back at the dwelling of the society with his umbrella:

"I honestly believe those are the most upright and sincere people I have ever met. There is not a particle of cant, of pretence, or sham about them, but they are genuine, through and through."

"I quite agree with you," responded the clergyman; "I was just thinking that they are to be envied the freedom they have earned to always say precisely what they mean. There must be an immense satisfaction in it."

"Yes," said the editor, "the most ridiculous thing in the world is the deference we pay to Mrs. Grundy."

CHAPTER XVIII.

MR. SCOTT'S DECISION.

As the year of Mr. Scott's probationary membership drew to a close he received a letter from his lady cousin, Mrs. Vincent, reminding him of his engagement to meet her and his other friends, to report his impressions of the Society of the Perfect Life, and his decision as to becoming a full or covenanting member. He replied, promising to be present on the appointed day, and immediately began his preparations for the journey. He had a long talk with Father Temple, in which they discussed future plans and prospects. The leader had never before been so full of courage and enthusiasm. He wished that he might live to see the whole world enjoying the benefits of his discoveries, looking forward to a time when friendly co-operation should take the place of selfish competition.

The members of the Society had
become strongly attached to Mr. Scott,
and at his leave-taking the salutations
were so affectionate and sincere as to
move him deeply. Quite a party went
over to the station to see him off.
George Stanley came forward to press
his hand and wish him prosperity.
Julia, Minette, and many others gave
him ample proofs of their regard.
Then he sprang up the steps into the
car and was whirled away to New
York. How strange it seemed to him
to find himself again in the atmosphere
of tobacco and whiskey-laden breaths,
and to begin paying out money for
everything he wanted! If he had
dropped down from another planet the
change could not have impressed him
more.

Behold him at length again seated in
the drawing-room of Mrs. Vincent's
handsome residence, prepared to discuss and explain all the features of the
new life. Mr. Vincent and the Rev.
Mr. Langford and his wife were also
present. Mrs. Vincent opened the con-

versation with the promptness and vivacity natural to her.

"Cousin George," she began, "our ideas of social reform have changed somewhat during the year that you have spent at the Society of the Perfect Life. We have been all reading up on the subject, and I hope you will not find us so ignorant in regard to it as we were a year ago. The Society you visited is becoming quite well known. We have read some of Mr. Temple's writings, and as far as religion is concerned, even Mr. Langford has to admit that he is pretty sound. We are not so sure about his social theories and practices, and have been waiting in some suspense to hear you report."

"It makes me happy to know that I am to have so friendly and sympathetic an audience," replied Mr. Scott. "How shall I make my report? Would you like to question me, or shall I give give a brief and succinct account of what I found there?"

"I should like to have Mr. Scott give us a clear, connected statement without interruptions," said Mr. Vincent. "If he fails to satisfy our curiosity on any point we can remember it, and after he has finished his story ask him questions."

"That will be the best way," said Mr. Langford; and as the ladies also signified their approval, Mr. Scott began:

"I will try to sketch the Society to you just as it would appear, and as it would impress you, if you were to go there.

"First, as to externals. Picture to yourselves a beautiful valley; on a commanding eminence in the midst of it, and surrounded by trees, lawns, and flower-gardens, stands a stately and well-proportioned edifice of brick, trimmed with granite. This edifice is designed for a unitary home for fifty or sixty ordinary-sized families, or about three hundred persons, men, women, and children; and it is full. It has only one kitchen, where the cooking is done for all; one dining-room, large enough to accommodate everyone; one laundry, and so on. There is a large Hall in the building, which serves at once as a chapel, a theater, and a family sitting-room. The Society owns broad fields, with orchards and vineyards, and busy factories. The most perfect order and neatness reign everywhere.

"Secondly, as to organization. All the property is owned in common; each member has a voice in deciding affairs, the women equally with the men; there is no friction, but the utmost harmony prevails. The Society is very successful in business, and the income is now ample. The members have the reputation of being perfectly truthful and honest in all their dealings. It is a common saying among their neighbors that the word of a member of the Society of the Perfect Life is as good as a bond. The banks are ready to lend them any sums of money they may desire, but they dislike debt.

"In regard to spiritual things, I consider them much in advance of the world. They live for each other instead of for themselves, and this makes a home the like of which was never seen before on earth. By the way, when I first told you about this society a year ago, Mr. Langford remarked that such socialistic movements were all alike, and all equally certain to end in failure. Permit me to point out to at the beginning of our talk the inaccuracy of this statement. The Society of the Perfect Life is unique, quite different from anything ever before attempted in the history of the world, so far as we know, and it must be judged by itself.

"As to the life I led there, while it seemed very strange to me at first, I fell into their ways quite readily. When I was hungry I went to the dining room, where I was abundantly fed ; yet I never paid any board-bill. When I wanted new clothes or new shoes I went to the society's tailor or shoemaker, and was fitted to my taste. When my clothes were done I did not even ask the price of them, but simply carried them away and put them on. Their cost was charged to the common

'Clothing Account.' In fact, I was not charged for anything while I was there, and actually did not receive nor pay out a cent of money for nearly a year. I worked several hours each day, but received no wages. My health was excellent ; I never felt better in my life. It was just like living in one's father's family with several hundred brothers and sisters, all nice, refined, lovable people.

"The fashions in vogue at the society are quite different from ours, but I found them sensible and attractive. I brought with me some photographs of the buildings and of the members, thinking you would like to see them."

"Indeed, we would," cried the ladies in concert. "You were very good to think of that."

Mr. Scott went to a side-table and took up a package which he had previously placed there. He quietly undid it, while the others drew their chairs close up to him. There were several photographs of the dwelling and factories. taken from various points of

view ; others represented a large group
of members on the lawn, with Father
Temple standing in their midst; Minette
singing on the stage in the Hall, with
Hugo and Julia playing her accompani-
ment; a group of the smallest children,
with their little wheelbarrows and
wagons, playing under the tall pine
trees ; and a typical " fruit-bee." There
were also cabinet portraits of Father
Temple, Mother Temple, Julia Fordham, and half-a-dozen others.

"I will make these part of my
report," said Mr. Scott, as he handed
them out.

The pictures were passed around
from hand to hand, and eagerly scanned.

"What a strange style of dress!"
exclaimed Mrs. Langford. "Yet it
does not look nearly as unattractive as
I had supposed it would from the de-
scription. But these are all girls ; did
none of the women stand in the
group?"

"Many of those you see are women
of thirty and forty, and some of them
even older," replied Mr. Scott.

"Can that be possible? They appear like girls, with their short hair and short dresses."

"Yes, it gives a much more youthful appearance than do your fashions."

"Who is this girl?" asked Mrs. Vincent, holding up a photograph.

"Her name is Julia Fordham; she is the same who is playing the piano in the other picture. What do you think of her?"

"She would be beautiful if she were properly dressed and had not cut off her hair. Are you specially interested in her?"

"She is a very lovable girl," replied Mr. Scott. "But let us not be drawn away from the order we laid down.

"I wish to bring clearly to your minds the fact that this Society has now been in existence long enough to demonstrate fully its completeness and its many advantages. The people composing it were only a fair average slice of our population, if I may use such an expression; therefore I think their system capable of general adop-

tion.   You may consider my report
finished, and proceed to question me."

The Rev. Mr. Langford had been
examining the photographs very
thoughtfully, particularly those of the
people. He looked at Father Temple's
portrait a long time, and it was evident
that he was in a severe exercise of mind.
The pictures, and what Mr. Scott had
reported, had impressed upon him the
fact that the work accomplished by the
Society was too great, and its obvious
lessons too important, to be pooh-
poohed away.   It was difficult for him
to change opinions which he had once
formed, but he was an honest, fair-
minded man, and he knew that we must
all be judged by our fruits. The fruits
of the Society were so evidently good
as to compel in him a feeling of respect ;
yet it cost him a struggle to admit to
himself that a movement so at variance
with the established order of things
could be worthy of consideration.

"Mr. Scott," he said at length, with
great seriousness of manner, "I have
the fullest confidence in your integrity

and truthfulness, and I want to ask you, right here and now, whether it is your honest belief that this Mr. Temple and his followers are good, moral people? I want you to answer me that without any mental reservation whatever, but in the plainest possible way."

"I certainly do consider them good, moral people," replied Mr. Scott. "They are the best and most unselfish people I have ever personally known."

"But they have discarded marriage, and are living together in one great home. Now, though they may be kind-hearted and unselfish towards each other as you say, do you consider them to be leading pure and moral lives?"

"I do, as I have already told you. But you need not take my unsupported word for it. You ought to know enough about human nature to understand that if these people were leading lives of hypocrisy, preaching the doctrine that we must all be saved from sin, while they practiced sensual self-indulgence, they could not have lived together in harmony for a single week. Jealous ies and quarrels would have sprung up such as would inevitably have disrupted the Society. The fact that they have gone on peacefully and harmoniously for so many years is the strongest possible proof that they have good consciences before God. I should be compelled to admit that from my knowledge of human nature, even if I had never seen them; but having lived with them for a year I can add the most emphatic personal testimony to their uprightness."

"It is almost incomprehensible to me how such a system can exist," said Mr. Langford. "My observations of human nature lead me to distrust it pretty thoroughly. I cannot see how, the rest of the world being under the dominion of sin, this particular three hundred should be saved from it as you claim."

"The explanation is simple," replied Mr. Scott. "Man has not power in himself to overcome the evil one, but God has that power. As soon as we learn to let the spirit of God control us in every affair of life we are saved from temptation and from sin. We become filled with an exceeding great love of God and of His Son, such that no other thing is half so attractive to us. Then nothing can tempt us to do any-thing which would be displeasing to God, or which would shut off the cur-rent of His love. It is not probable that the three hundred persons who now compose the Society of the Per-fect Life would have achieved this spiritual victory if they had remained in their isolated, worldly homes, and had never met Father Temple. He is the medium of the good, heavenly spirit to his followers. It is he who upholds them in the attitude of faith, trust, and waiting on inspiration. I do not know that all those people are yet sufficiently well-established in their spiritual self-conquest, or that they might not relapse into tempta-tions and selfishness if Father Temple's controlling influence were removed, or if they were to go back into the world again."

"That statement brings the matter

more within my comprehension," said
Mr. Langford. " Mr. Temple is evidently a very remarkable man. It follows from what you say, does it not,
that the system he has established is
not capable of general adoption, except
as such inspired leaders can be found ?"

"Yes, the system is dependent on
such leadership. There must also be a
change of heart and a putting away of
selfishness before mankind can realize
such great blessings as broad unity and
close fellowship with large numbers."

" I do not care to ask any more questions," said Mr. Langford. "The
whole matter seems to me to hinge on
the character of the people and of the
lives they lead. If the new system
makes better men and women than the
old one, then it is a better system, and
it is useless to contend otherwise.
What you say satisfies me on that point,
and I do not feel like making small,
carping objections to their way of life.
If it is possible to adopt better social
forms, such as will shut out evil influences and invite in good ones, I, as a

minister of the gospel, ought to welcome them; and I can readily understand that such homes, where none of
the worst temptations could enter, and
where each member was watchful of
the good of all the others, would do
much to elevate mankind."

"The important thing is to get rid of
selfishness," said Mr. Scott. "No
social reform will amount to much that
does not accomplish that."

"One feature of the new system
struck me as being really admirable,"
said Mrs. Langford. "Mr. Scott tells
us that the women have an equal voice
with the men in deciding all matters.
Does that hold good in regard to business moves, questions of investment,
the election of managers, and so on?"

"Certainly," replied Mr. Scott; "the
women are made perfectly free to propose new moves, to take part in discus-
sions, and to vote on all questions.
Their votes count for as much as, the
men's."

"That is excellent," said Mrs. Langford. "It tempts me to wish to join
the society myself."

Mr. Langford looked at his worthy spouse and smiled. He had grown used to her enthusiasm for women's rights.

Mr. Scott continued :

" A year under Father Temple's instruction has given me a new comprehension of the bearing our lives have on the question of saving our souls. I have heard plenty of good doctrine preached on this subject in the churches, but I have not seen it practised before in a saving way. The salvation of our souls is unquestionably the supremely important object, to which all our efforts in this life should be directed. ' What shall it profit a man if he gain the whole world and lose his own soul ?' That is a plain, sensible question. Now let us suppose for a moment that we can look down on the world as the angels do ; what should we see ? Nations armed with soldiers, cruisers, and cannon, watching each other like savage bulldogs, each one ready to go to war and to subjugate another whenever it can be caught at a disadvantage ; men and women everywhere engaged in a fierce strife of competition for the possession of power and wealth, the strong crushing the weak, some living in gross luxury, others starving; prisons filled with those who have committed crimes; asylums filled with those who have lost their reason in the mad rush of modern life; poorhouses filled with wretched paupers; a large police force maintained in every city in order that honest citizens may go about without being killed and robbed; married life marked by divorces, jealousies, and murders 'without number; thousands of children begotten while their parents were intoxicated, and by criminals; the whole system of human propagation as unscientific as possible. That is what we should see. It is not a pleasant or refined picture, is it?"

"I declare, cousin George," exclaimed Mrs. Vincent, "you have a strange way of holding things up to us! There is a great deal of good in the world as well as evil."

"That is quite true, but must we not

get rid of the evil before we shall be fit to enter heaven ?   It seems to me that men are so swamped in the miseries of the old social system that they have grown indifferent to the question of salvation."

" The fact is we haven't time to attend to it properly," said Mr. Vincent. " Most men have to give their whole time and strength to earning their bread and butter.   They go to church once a week, perhaps, and let such good men as Mr. Langford talk to them for an hour.   That is all the attention they can afford to give to the subject."

" Why, Reginald, please don't talk so ; it sounds positively irreligious," said Mrs. Vincent.

" But is it not true ?"

" Unhappily it is true of too many," said Mr. Langford.   " It is an awful state of things.   Our only hope is in God's mercy."

" I do not think you realize how much evil is protected and fostered by these old institutions, such as the private ownership of property, and marriage," said Mr. Scott. "It is true that in the old system men are compelled to strive with their fellows for the means of subsistence. They have to look out for their wives and little ones, and that seems a worthy motive. But acquisitiveness becomes a passion, cold and cruel, willing to ruin others for its own gain. It hardens the heart and deadens the spiritual nature. I once saw an eagle catch and devour an honest hen. It swooped down upon its defenceless prey, seizing it alive in its horrid claws. Then with its great, curved beak it stripped the feathers from the side of its screaming victim, and with one strong blow of its bill penetrated the abdomen and drew forth the steaming entrails to devour them. It is a dreadful sight thus to see a strong, soulless creature destroy a defenceless one. There is no trace of sympathy, no hesitation, but a calm, deliberate rending of the victim. But have you not seen equally cold-blooded and cruel things done in what is called business'? I have known men with

enormous capital to deliberately plan
the financial ruin of those less fortified,
utterly regardless of the suffering and
want they were bringing on innocent
mothers and children. Such soulless
men are the eagles of society."

"That is a common sight," said Mr.
Vincent. "It is one of the incidents of
competition."

"Contrast now, if you will," continued Mr. Scott, "the two systems I
have pictured to you. In the Society
of the Perfect Life not a single crime
has been committed during a quarter of
a century; nor has there been an instance of poverty, want, or neglect. It
is a state where there is no strife nor
intrigue, but where brotherly love and
Christian fellowship reign. Above all,
every individual there has ample time
to attend to his salvation. That is his
first business, morning, noon, and night.
If all the world would put away selfishness and adopt that system, there would
no longer be any need of politicians,
lawyers, soldiers, or policemen. Everyone would do his share of honest toil

but none would need to labor more than three or four hours daily to produce all that was required. The rest of the time could be devoted to improving pursuits and innocent recreations. It would be a system of universal co-operation, with love as the medium of exchange.

"Looking on the two systems, can you ask me in which I shall choose to cast my lot? Assuredly, I shall return to the little Heaven on Earth, where I have been so happy, and where I have learned so much of the deeper philosophy of life."

THE END.